To Ja

Keep reading.

THE GUARDIANS OF
ELIJAH'S FIRE

THE GUARDIANS OF ELIJAH'S FIRE

FRANK L. COLE

BONNEVILLE BOOKS

AN IMPRINT OF CEDAR FORT, INC.

SPRINGVILLE, UTAH

ISBN 13: 978-1-4621-1057-5

Published by Bonneville Books, an imprint of Cedar Fort, Inc., 2373 W. 700 S., Springville, UT 84663
Distributed by Cedar Fort, Inc., www.cedarfort.com

Cover design by Danie Romrell and Brian Halley
Cover illustration by Mark McKenna
Cover design © 2012 by Lyle Mortimer
Edited and typeset by Kelley Konzak

Printed in the United States of America

10 9 8 7 6 5 4 3 2 1

Printed on acid-free paper

To Michael, the wizard.
Fahroom, my friend. *Fahroom!*

1

Even with the door latched on my mailbox at the Nordwall Student Center, I could see it brimming with all sorts of goodies. The colored corners of envelopes stuck out from the mail slot as I eagerly inserted my key, and a barrage of birthday cards and small packages toppled from the opening. I had just turned fifteen years old, and in one week I would take my learner's permit exam and would be legally allowed behind the wheel of a car. Of course, there would have to be a licensed driver in the vehicle with me until I turned sixteen, but I would be driving.

The fading sunlight shone through the Student Center window, and the bell tower on the grounds of the quad released several echoing chimes. It was five o'clock, and my stomach instinctively rumbled. I had been too busy with homework and studying to eat breakfast or lunch. After shoveling the cards and packages into my backpack, I headed out toward the refectory for dinner.

Later that evening, tons of cash, gift certificates, and

birthday cards with corny messages lay strewn about my bed. My parents had already sent me the bulk of my gifts a few days earlier on my actual birthday, but that didn't stop them from sending me more. Only one package remained for me to open. I stared at the small, rectangular box wrapped with brown paper, turning it over in my hands in search of a return address. There was none. It felt slightly heavy as I shook the package and the contents shifted.

"Oh yes!" I pumped my fist in celebration. My dad had hinted he would be sending me a new smartphone, and this package seemed just the right size. I couldn't wait to see how this one compared to my friend Trendon's latest electronic contraption. As I tore off the paper, I felt my spirits fade. It sure didn't look like a smartphone package. The cardboard box was fiercely covered with yellow packing tape.

"What is this?" I dolefully whispered as I fished a pair of scissors out of my desk and removed the wrapper.

Inside the box I discovered two relatively thin, leather-bound books. The covers were well worn, and most of the gilding had faded on the edges of the pages. There were no titles or authors' names on either book, just blank covers carrying a faint scent of mildew. Carefully, I opened one of them. The writing was in English, and the pages were broken up into chapters and verses. It was the first book of Kings, typically found in the Bible. I thumbed through each of the pages, looking for notes or an inserted message, but found nothing. An examination of the second book yielded a similar result.

It contained the second book of Kings.

Why had somebody sent me books from the Bible? Instantly, I felt a ripple of excitement in my chest even more than when I had believed the package to hold a smartphone.

A mysterious box. No return address. Biblical verses. I knew of only one person who would send me such a gift.

"Dorothy!" I giggled. I hadn't heard from Dorothy Holcomb, my independent archaeology teacher, for quite a while. In fact, the last time we spoke had been in the hospital just after the incident in the Philippines. Dorothy and Cabarles had made plans to move the Tebah Stick to a safer location, and I had wondered when she would surface again. Life at the Roland and Tesh Private School for the Advanced was not the same with-out her. I pulled out my good luck charm and gave it a kiss. Dorothy had given me a beautiful stone necklace to wear, which happened to be a locator stone. If it hadn't been for the necklace, both Trendon and I would've drowned in an endless room of foul water. I never went anywhere without it. Knowing Dorothy had been the one to send me the books, I examined them more closely.

It had been over a year since my last Sunday School class, and trying to remember the events in the books of Kings proved to be slightly difficult—but only slightly. As I flipped through the pages, searching for key words and names, my memory returned. The first book of Kings held the story of Elijah. A memory of one of the cross-stitched Bible verses hanging in Dorothy's apart-ment rushed into my mind.

1 Kings 18:11.

I found the verse and read it silently.

And now thou sayest, Go, tell thy lord, Behold, Elijah is here.

Immediately bumps rose on my forearms and I shivered. "Creepy," I whispered.

Dorothy had a notorious nature for sending hidden messages to her students, particularly to me. I checked the cover for any secret compartments, remembering how she had once placed a note underneath the leather binding of a dictionary. After a few sturdy tugs on the corners, I feared I might damage the books and gave up on the idea. I looked for pencil markings by some of the verses or notes in the margin. Surely she would've highlighted a few verses for me to read. After a few moments of searching, I found a couple of ink marks circling four different verses. The first two were in the first book of Kings: chapter three, verses five and eight. The last two verses were in the second book: chapter three, verse six, and chapter four, verse five.

I read each of them, expecting a familiar phrase to stand out, but none of the verses made any sense. At least not yet. I would need more time to study, but I knew I could find the answer. With a sigh, I slid the two mysterious items into my backpack and got ready for bed.

Just after two in the morning, I woke up panicked from a nightmare. Though I couldn't remember the details, the dream had definitely bothered me. Since the Philippines, I often stirred in the middle of the night due to some dream. Sometimes I could remember them. Whether I found myself trapped in a cave with Trendon or being followed by those creatures guarding the Tebah Stick, they always seemed so real until I awoke and could think rationally. I sat up and rubbed my eyes. It had only been a dream. As with the others, it was harmless.

At that moment I realized I wasn't alone. Slowly, I turned as something crouching in the corner slid out of view. My room was too dark to make out its features, but it wouldn't matter anyway. A thick mist seemed to cling to its body, shielding it from my eyes.

"Hello?" I whimpered. It moved, shrinking away from my voice. I had encountered this creature before, and it had stamped its mark on my memory. The last time I had seen it, I had held the Tebah Stick, which placed the monster under my control. What would it do now that I had nothing in my possession to defend myself against it?

Its eyes opened, illuminating the darkness with a dull glow, and I screamed. I shot my hand out to switch on the lamp on my bedside table, and the light instantly flooded the room. The creature in the corner vanished. Head still hazy from what I hoped was only a dream, I swung my feet off the bed and walked briskly to where I had seen it. Only a small pile of blankets and my backpack rested in the corner. By now my heart thudded a steady rhythm in my chest. With my jaw clenched, ready for the worst, I kicked aside the blankets and then took my search to the closet. As I had hoped, I found only luggage and a few pairs of shoes.

A sharp knock sounded at my door, and I jumped, clutching my chest.

"Amber, you all right?" The voice belonged to Sierra Pontiff, the dorm hall's resident assistant, whose bedroom sat right next to mine.

Releasing an exasperated sigh, I shook away my anxiety. "I'm fine," I answered, crossing the room to open the door. A tall girl wearing scrubs and slippers stared down at me. She held her arms crossed at her waist as I shrugged. "I just had a bad dream. I'm sorry."

"Every night this week, huh?" Sierra asked.

My cheeks reddened. Had I really done this that many times? What kind of weirdo was I turning into? "Yeah, I'm just stressed about school, that's all."

"Do you want to talk about it?"

Sierra had to be one of the most genuine people I'd ever met. If I really needed to talk to her, she'd listen. Would she believe me? Doubtful. But she would absolutely act as though she did.

"No, I'm fine. Really." I shook my head and yawned.

"You're sure?" Sierra's eyes narrowed, and she smiled. "I don't mind."

The phone on my desk started to ring. Both Sierra and I gasped, not expecting the sudden eruption, but then we both laughed. I glanced at my alarm clock.

"Is it really only 2:30?" I asked.

Sierra clicked her tongue. "Yeah, pretty late for a phone call. You better get that, but tell your boyfriend not to call past eleven next time."

"I don't have a boyfriend," I muttered.

Great, now Sierra thought I was staying up late to chat with some crush. I said good night, closed the door, and raced for the phone, already on its fifth ring.

"Hello?" I asked warily into the receiver. Who would be calling me this late?

Silence on the other end. No, not complete silence . . . I could hear breathing.

"Who is this?" My voice cracked.

No answer.

"Tell me who this is!" I demanded, this time in a forceful tone.

The next sounds sent ice through my veins. Though not spoken directly into the phone on the other end, I distinctly heard the guttural, choking sounds of someone speaking in a hideous language. I knew the sound, though I didn't understand the words.

"What do you want?" I tried to sound tough, but my whole body shook from fear. More choking sounds, like someone making noises from the back of his throat. They grew louder, almost desperate, and then . . .

"Amber." This new voice sounded younger and as though struggling to catch his breath.

"Joseph? Is that you?" The last time I had seen Joseph, he was badly injured in his Uncle Jasher's office. Though he had become my enemy when he betrayed me to his uncle, we had left on good terms, and I hoped things would turn out all right for him. Hearing him now on the phone, obviously forced to speak by Mr. Baeloc, made me realize the opposite had happened.

"What does he want? Has Baeloc hurt you?" I tried to

hold more control on my composure. Mr. Baeloc frightened me more than any other man I had ever met, but I felt more hatred for him than fear. I knew very little about him or his race of people called the Qedet, descendants from the Architects of the Tower of Babel, but I did know pure evil motivated his intentions. Trendon and I prevented the Tebah Stick from falling into his hands, which I knew didn't sit well with him.

"I'm all right. It's not what you think. Mr. Baeloc is not here with me," Joseph answered.

More guttural sounds in the background. More instruction. The voice sounded almost mechanical.

"Don't lie to me! I can hear him talking to you!" I shouted into the phone.

"No, listen, that's someone else. His name's Sherez, and he's a friend trying to help us."

"Help who? Don't trust him, Joseph. He's one of them!" I had wanted to speak with Joseph for quite some time, but not like this, and certainly not under these conditions.

"Sherez *is* a member of the Qedet, but he's not like the others. He thinks Mr. Baeloc has gone off the deep end, and he's trying to put a stop to him."

More choking from the voice, and despite Joseph's insistence of Sherez's legitimacy, I shivered from the sound. I absolutely hated that voice. No other sound produced the same effect on my insides like the unnatural chatter of the Architects.

"How are you understanding him?" I asked. I didn't think anyone but members of the Qedet could understand their awful language. Yet there was Joseph, apparently carrying on a conversation.

"He can write, Amber." Joseph chuckled lightly. "I'm just reading it off a piece of paper."

I squeezed the receiver, wanting so badly to know if this were legit. "This is crazy! You aren't thinking straight. How can you trust them? You need to . . ."

"Amber, we don't have much time!" Joseph snapped, cutting me off midsentence. "I'm taking a dangerous risk by making this call, so please let me finish."

I closed my mouth and exhaled through my nostrils. This was only a phone call. I could hang up at any second, which gave me control. If I felt Joseph try to brainwash me, I would simply end the call. Until then, I could hear him out. "Okay," I answered cautiously.

"Mr. Baeloc has stolen it back." The words echoed through the receiver. I knew what "it" was, but that was impossible. Dorothy and Cabarles had moved the Tebah Stick months ago. No one should be able to find it that quickly.

"He has the Tebah Stick? No, he doesn't!" I said, my voice harsh with finality.

"I've seen it myself. Just a few days ago, he returned, and he has it."

"Then it has to be a fake." Of course it was a fake. Joseph had never seen the Tebah Stick. How could he know what it really looked like? "He's lying to you. There's no way he could've . . ."

"It's not a fake!" Joseph shouted. I felt my hold on the phone slacken. Then he spoke softer. "Trust me. It's not a fake."

I took a deep breath and tried to think through this. If they did indeed have the scepter, then we were all in great danger. Yes, it certainly seemed impossible, but on the off chance Joseph was right . . . "Okay, why are you calling me? What do you want me to do about it?"

Sherez's ghastly voice growled instruction, and I cringed. Joseph remained silent while Sherez spoke and then finally said, "There's still time, but not much. They haven't figured out how to use it yet, but they will."

"Then call the police. It doesn't make any sense to call me. I can't help you." I ran my fingers through my hair, sweat dripping down my forehead. I wanted nothing more than to wake up and realize I had dreamed the entire phone call.

"Baeloc owns the police here. Come on, Amber, you know that," Joseph chided.

"Where's here? Where are you calling from?"

"Syria."

I blinked as world geography processed in my brain. My voice cracked with disbelief. "What are you doing there?"

"There's no time to explain. I called you because I think you may be in danger, and I don't want to be responsible for this. You've got to get help. I'll do what I can to stop them."

"Why am I in danger?" I asked, growing in alarm.

"Things aren't going according to plan, and they're going to try something else."

Joseph's sincerity troubled me. He sounded honestly concerned about my well-being. As touching as that was, it equally frustrated me. I shouldn't be in any danger. If Joseph was right, Baeloc had scored the victory. He could bury any bad blood geared at me with knowing he had won in the end.

"Fine. I'll try to get a message out to Dorothy."

Joseph breathed, hesitating. "That's the other thing. I don't know if you should be involving her."

"Don't be ridiculous! Of course I should involve Dorothy. She knows all about the Tebah Stick."

'You need to be careful around her. I know you don't trust me, but I . . ."

"She's one of the only people I can trust!"

Sherez's voice rose with excitement in the background.

"Amber, I've got to go!" And with that, the receiver went dead.

I stood staring at the phone as though it were a venomous snake. Mr. Baeloc had the Tebah Stick? Why hadn't Dorothy made contact with me? Did she even know? Without thinking, I dialed another number. On the other end, the line rang seven times before connecting with an answering machine. I hung up and dialed the same number again. More ringing and another click of the machine connecting. On my third try, just before the seventh ring, I heard the receiver pick up and someone growl on the other end.

"What do you want?" Trendon's voice groaned into the phone.

I wasted no time in filling in my friend.

2

Something had changed inside of me. I never thought there would be any problems with holding the Tebah Stick, and I only did what I thought would keep it safe. Lately, I began to wonder if I made a bad choice. The artifact contained so much power, and I felt hollow without it. Dorothy Holcomb, the only person I felt understood my situation, had yet to return from abroad.

Not knowing the activity happening outside the walls of my school drove me crazy. Was Dorothy involved in another dangerous assignment? Was her secret organization, the Seraphic Scroll, making any progress at keeping the Tebah Stick hidden? And perhaps the one question bothering me the most, what were Kendell Jasher and Mr. Baeloc planning?

Later that evening, Lisa Hardgrave, one of my best friends, met me outside my dorm hall, and we headed off campus to meet Trendon for dinner. Friday night study groups were not their idea of fun, but they agreed to meet as long as it took place off campus so as to appear we could have a life outside of school.

The weekend always brought a ton of students down to the main stretch of restaurants. While some kids had their licenses, most of us walked the mile and a half to Burdette Street, where you could find anything from Greek and Indian food to movie theaters and miniature golf. Lisa and I walked amid a group of our sophomore friends, heading to different destinations. I passed Sierra on the sidewalk, and she shoved me playfully in the shoulder.

"Hey you! Did you finally get back to sleep last night?" she asked with a smile.

I laughed. "Yeah, went right to bed." That was a total lie. Shadows with eyes. Joseph in cahoots with the Architects. Not the type of thought process that induced sleep.

"Does your boyfriend know the rules now?" Sierra asked. "He's not going to make it a habit to call you every night now, is he?" She said all this in a friendly, nonthreatening manner, but I knew she stuck to the rules and held everyone in her dorm accountable.

"No, I sure hope not." I forced another laugh as Sierra and her friends crossed the road to the Roller Restaurant. If only she knew how badly I never wanted another phone call like that again.

"Boyfriend?" Lisa tugged on my arm as we crossed the parking lot of Papa B's Burgers.

"Never mind," I said, shaking my head.

I had never been much of a burger fan, but Trendon had insisted on picking the location of our meeting.

"Why do you always pick this place, Trendon?" Lisa asked as the two of us sat down next to him in the booth. I dropped my backpack onto the ground at my feet and unwrapped my sandwich.

Trendon looked up and grinned, mustard clinging to the corners of his mouth. "Isn't it obvious?" he asked with a mouthful of burger. "You said you wanted cozy and private, right? What's more private than this place?" He swung his hand in a sweeping gesture. Packed with students, families, and everything in between, Papa B's was anything but private. It could easily have been the most popular hangout spot in town.

"I can't stay long, guys," Lisa said, looking away with guilt. "I'm going with Michael to the movies at seven."

I wanted to tell her she needed to take this seriously, but I knew it would be no use. Lisa began dating Michael right at the beginning of the fall term. Though boys always hung around outside of her dorm, showing off and basically acting like idiots to get her attention, Michael was her first real boyfriend. He seemed nice enough, but I hated how distracted he made her, especially with our group.

"Okay, this will have to do, but keep your voices down," I whispered.

Trendon wiped his mouth with the back of his hand, then noticed the mustard and licked it off as well. "I think he's lying."

"Joseph? Yeah, maybe," I said. Joseph had proven to be an excellent deceiver. He fooled everyone at Roland and Tesh of his true identity for several years. And just because he eventually helped us out in Istanbul, it didn't mean he couldn't start back up to his old ways. "But why would he call me and lie about that?"

"Mr. Baeloc's forcing him." Trendon sucked on his straw and slurped his drink with no care of how loud it sounded. After finally coming up for air, he continued. "They're fishing."

"Fishing?" Lisa's head swiveled slightly from the window.

"Yeah, fishing. Obviously they're miffed because they can't seem to find the dumb stick, and now they're casting their lines in to see if they can get someone to bite. If they can get Amber to believe them, even to trust old Joseph, maybe she'll slip up and reveal some information they could use on their hunt." Trendon's eye gleamed with pride. He sure believed he knew what he was talking about.

I considered his idea for a moment, but it didn't stick long. "I don't think that's it. These people are pretty smart. Wouldn't they know I didn't have the Tebah Stick and that Dorothy would've taken it somewhere safe by now?"

"They're not that smart," Trendon said, muffling a burp. "You and I got the best of them, didn't we?" He winked, and I couldn't help but raise the corners of my lips in a semismile. I then thought back to the sound of the awful chattering voice from the phone call and rubbed my arms to ward off the shivers. Maybe it hadn't been Mr. Baeloc and Joseph was telling the truth about Sherez being on his side. Regardless, their voices had the same cringe-inducing effect as fingernails on a chalkboard.

"Okay, let's consider the other possibility." I lowered my voice even more. "What if he's telling the truth? What then?"

Trendon scrunched up his nose and stared at his burger wrappers. Lisa had turned her attention away from the window but still seemed disinterested in the conversation. I waited for a response, but no one seemed ready to give one.

"Guys, if they have the artifact, we have to do something," I said.

Trendon shook his head. "Nope. You're wrong. We've done enough. Let's say they somehow miraculously stole back the stick." Since the Philippines, Trendon always referred to the Tebah Stick as "the stick." It seemed disrespectful, but he wouldn't change his ways. "Again, I think it's highly unlikely and that you're just giving too much credit to those imbeciles, but I'll go along with this for a moment. The smart thing to do would be to get in touch with Dorothy and tell her little club all about it. And then leave it for them to handle." He scratched the tip of his nose with his finger.

"I agree," Lisa said, glancing down at her watch to check the time. We still had a good half hour before Michael picked her up, but I could tell she had checked out of the conversation a while ago.

I sighed. "You're right. How do we get in touch with Dorothy?"

Trendon gasped. "Are you actually going to listen

to me?" He shook his head and blinked his eyes with a baffled expression.

"Yes," I groaned. "As much as I hate to admit it, we're not cut out for this, and the best thing to do would be to let Dorothy handle it. Oh, stop with the goofy smile already!" Trendon couldn't stop smiling from ear to ear. "Do you think you can find her?"

He pulled out his phone and went to work hacking his way back into Dorothy's life. If anyone could find her exact location, Trendon could. I thought I'd seen his greatest work last spring, but over the summer, Trendon graduated to a whole new level of hacker. While he labored with his search, I slid over next to Lisa.

"I almost forgot." I removed the two leather books from my backpack and handed them to her. "Look what someone mysteriously sent me for my birthday. There was no return address on the package."

Rubbing her eyes, she glanced with little interest at my books. "That's neat. Who do you think sent them?"

Neat? Just neat? There was a time when Lisa became as excited as I did about old books. "They're the first and second books of Kings." I handed the books to Trendon. "I was wondering if you guys gave them to me."

"Crappy old books?" Trendon asked, flipping open to the cover page and then shrugging as he returned his attention to his phone. "However did you guess?"

"Then it can only mean one other person. Dorothy sent them. Which means there has to be some significance to them. An archaeological significance." I licked my thumb and carefully turned the pages. "Look, she marked only four verses total between the two books. They must be important, but I can't figure out why."

Lisa humored me for a moment and read the verses.

1 Kings 3:5—In Gibeon the Lord appeared to Solomon in a dream by night: and God said, Ask what I shall give thee.

1 Kings 3:8—And thy servant is in the midst of thy people which thou hast chosen, a great people, that cannot be numbered nor counted for multitude.

2 Kings 3:6—And king Jehoram went out of Samaria the same time, and numbered all Israel.

2 Kings 4:5—So she went from him, and shut the door upon her and upon her sons, who brought the vessels to her; and she poured out.

"They don't make any sense to me," she said after finishing. "One of them is talking about Solomon, and I faintly remember him from church."

"I know, so why would Dorothy want me to read about Solomon or any of these weird names? It really is a mystery!" I loved how confusing the verses seemed. It meant I needed to dig deeper and the answer wouldn't be simply discovered on the surface. Those were the best kinds of mysteries only Dorothy knew how to provide.

Trendon looked from his phone and smirked. "Sounds like absolute garbage if you ask me. Those were the only verses circled?"

"As far as I can tell."

He put his research on hold for a moment to reread the verses. "Yep, I was right . . . garbage. It looks to me like someone accidentally marked them."

"Come on, you know you don't believe that," I said.

"It's a puzzle. All we need to do is put our heads together to find the pieces."

"Sounds like fun, but I don't think I'm cut out for this serious archaeology stuff anymore," Lisa said. "Michael thinks it's silly."

"You think I'm silly too, don't you?" Closing the books, I dropped them once again in my backpack.

Lisa stared back at me. "I didn't say that. Part of me thinks it's all just a game. That, yeah, maybe there really are important artifacts out there and they're probably worth a lot of money, but I don't know if I can believe they possess power."

"Lisa, I felt that power. I had total control over those creatures."

Lisa frowned. "And that's another thing. I don't think I believe all those things really happened to you guys in the Philippines."

My mouth dropped open slightly. I didn't want to make a big fuss over our conversation, but I couldn't just sit there and not defend what I knew to be true. "What do you mean by that? Of course it happened. I didn't make it up. We really saw those things, and we barely survived. Trendon will vouch for it, and so will Dorothy." We looked at Trendon. Without looking up from his iPhone, Trendon bared his teeth, mimicking the mouths of the creatures we encountered guarding the Tebah Stick.

"Yeah . . . maybe." Lisa smiled, but I knew she didn't believe me.

"So, what you're saying is we just imagined being

attacked? And that Trendon's injury was just a figment of our imaginations?"

"Amber." Lisa's voice sounded sympathetic. "I didn't mean it like that. All I'm saying . . ."

But before she could finish her thought, several customers at the front of the line near the registers started a commotion. A woman's voice rose high above the rest.

"Is this a game?" she shouted. A fight broke out, a couple of men grappled with each other, and several kids dropped to the floor, shielding their heads. What were they fighting about? Had someone cut line? I rose to my knees in the chair for a better look. One of the men, a restaurant employee, was trying to wrestle a machine gun free from the other, a stranger in a hooded black jacket.

Customers scattered as the man in the jacket pulled the gun free and smashed the butt against the employee's nose. He crumpled over, unconscious, and everyone began to scream, shielding their heads as they fled from the checkout counter.

3

"Get your heads down!" Trendon reached over to shove our heads below the booth table and crowded in next to us as we watched the horror unfold. "They're robbing Papa B's?" he asked, sounding as though struggling to suppress laughter.

"Shut up!" Lisa whispered. "We have the worst luck ever!"

Gunfire erupted as two men fired into the ceiling. More screaming. Trays dropped, spilling soda and ice and splattering food and condiments everywhere. Children were clinging to their parents, confused and scared. Some people headed for the exits but quickly turned once they saw the way blocked by the gunmen.

"Everyone get down on the ground!" one of them shouted in a thick, accented voice. Was he Hispanic? No, something else. Something all too familiar. I couldn't call myself a linguist, but I recognized the diction in the man's throat and recalled the voices of my captors from Mr. Jasher's mansion in Istanbul. There was no mistaking it. They were speaking with Turkish accents.

Around us, people fell to the floor, cowering beneath the tables. I grabbed Trendon's arm and pointed to his phone, but he didn't have time to dial the police.

"Push your cell phones out on the floor in the middle. Do it now!" came the next instruction. Everyone around us quickly complied, but Trendon tucked his into his pocket. Leave it to him to go to dangerous means protecting his phone. Lisa and I tossed our phones out with the dozens of others in the pile. "Now, everyone stay calm and quiet," he instructed. "This will only take a moment."

Were these men really just desperate criminals hoping to score some cash off of Papa B's? It seemed highly unlikely. I knew this was no coincidence. The men began checking under each table. They hadn't reached ours yet, and I chanced whispering to the others.

"We've got to get out of here!"

"Well, no duh," Trendon fired back. "How are we going to do that?"

"They're not here just to rob us," I said. "I'd bet anything they're working for Kendell Jasher."

"Ah, crud!" Trendon rolled his eyes with disgust.

I closed my eyes, trying to devise some sort of plan, but time ran out as a face peered below the table. The man had tan, heavily pocked skin and a grotesque spiderweb tattoo on his neck, covering his Adam's apple. A smile broke out across his lips, revealing missing teeth. Looking back over his shoulder, he muttered something to his partner, then stared back directly at me.

"Ms. Amber Rawson?" he asked. I didn't answer, and his smile widened. "Come with me, please." He held out his hand.

There had to be another way. I couldn't just give up and allow him to take me. Not after all the close calls I had already managed to escape. Before I could react, the man snatched my collar and forced me out from under the table. Lisa yelped and clasped her hand over her mouth in shock.

"Hey, moron! Leave her alone!" Trendon shouted, but they ignored him. Did they really think I still had the Tebah Stick? That couldn't be the reason. Maybe they had been listening in on my conversation with Joseph last night.

The man with the spiderweb tattoo probed me forward, directing me through the narrow walkways between the restaurant tables. Inwardly, I bombarded myself with insults, ashamed of how quickly I had been captured. I had let the Society of the Seraphic Scroll down.

"Stay down!" the man behind me shouted. "I said stay down!" Then he released an earsplitting scream of pain and fell into me, pushing me forward. I had no idea what was happening. Amid the struggle, I glanced over my shoulder and gasped as Trendon locked arms with the man with the spiderweb tattoo, trying to wrestle his machine gun free. Jutting out of the man's leg was Trendon's pocketknife stabbed deep into his calf muscle.

"Boy, you don't know what you're doing!" the man shouted.

"Trendon, are you crazy? They'll shoot you!" I shouted. But he didn't listen to me. My eyes darted up to the other gunman, the one aiming his weapon at Trendon. Everything slowed down in my mind, and I knew if I didn't create some sort of distraction, he would kill Trendon right in front of me. Without a second's hesitation, I flung myself in front of the gun. A tense moment passed, where I saw his finger on the trigger and I closed my eyes awaiting the bullet. Instead, he eased off the trigger and pointed the barrel away from me.

From behind me, the struggle continued. I couldn't tell who had gained the advantage, but although he acted lazy, I'd seen Trendon do amazing things when his adrenaline took hold. I heard a sharp thud, and glancing down at my feet, I saw the gunman's limp arm flop next to me.

"Drop it!" the man in front shouted at Trendon, who now held the machine gun.

"You dr-drop it!" Trendon stammered in response. I felt his hand grip my shoulder and move me out of the way as the two of them squared off with their weapons aimed at each other. This was something straight out of some bizarre nightmare. How did Trendon do that? I was shocked and impressed but now feared Trendon's luck would run out. He wouldn't really pull the trigger, and the man obviously sensed this.

"Put it down, kid," the man said. "Don't be stupid."

Trendon swallowed. "Look, I'm not dropping my gun, and you're not taking Amber, so maybe you and your buddy should . . . uh . . . skedaddle on out of here.

And give me back my pocketknife while you're at it."

"Trendon, how's this going to work?" I asked. Someone would have to surrender their weapon.

"Don't know, but don't ask me that right now," Trendon grumbled.

The restaurant door opened with the clinking sound of the welcoming bell. Trendon kept his eyes glued to the man in front of him, but I managed a quick glance toward the door. Kendell Jasher entered, followed by two more men with guns. He wore a pale green sports jacket over a white, collarless T-shirt, and dark green slacks. Striding in confidently, he smiled at the scene unfolding in the restaurant. My stomach tightened as my worst fears were confirmed.

"Oh my goodness," Jasher said, clucking his tongue. "What a mess. Amber, Trendon." He nodded to each of us. "It's been too long." He then said something sharply in Turkish, and the man squaring off with Trendon reluctantly lowered his weapon.

"I arrived just in time, wouldn't you agree?" Mr. Jasher glowered disappointingly at the man cradling his wounded calf muscle. "Victor, who did that to you?"

Victor scowled and nodded sideways at Trendon.

Kendell covered his mouth and feigned a gasp. He then brought his hands together in applause. "Bravo, my friend. Victor is one of my most skilled soldiers. Or so he tells me." He took a few steps closer to us. "Now, enough of this charade. We need to talk in a more private location."

"Nu-uh, buddy." Trendon pointed the gun at Jasher. "We're not listening to you."

"Lisa, get up here," I said. I reached out and snagged my backpack from the floor as she scrambled out from under the table.

"Come now, Trendon, you wouldn't shoot me, would you?" Jasher asked.

"Self-defense, puke face!" Trendon answered scathingly. "Try me."

Jasher's eyes narrowed momentarily but then brightened with amusement. "Where are you going to go?" He looked around, his lower lip curling down innocently. He then held out his hand and calmly patted the air in front of him. "Let's take it easy, shall we? There's no need for violence. It's not my first choice in any situation. As much as I've been looking forward to catching up with you, Trendon, this doesn't involve you. You're free to go. And you, Lisa isn't it?" He smiled at Lisa. She shivered, tears plopping from her eyes and smearing her mascara. "How lovely. I see no need to drag you into these trivialities. You have my permission to leave as well." He motioned to the exit, wiggling his fingers like writhing snakes. "I just need to have a simple conversation with Amber for a bit." He pressed his hand against his chest and closed his eyes. "I only wish to help her."

Trendon kept his hand on the trigger but reached sideways to pluck a French fry from a plastic serving tray. "Nice try, dipstick, but she's not going anywhere with you." He chomped down on the fry and smacked his lips obnoxiously.

Jasher made a pouting face. "So I guess this is what you would call a standoff. What's your next move?

26

You're not planning on going to Dorothy, are you? That would be a big mistake."

"Right, we should just go with you because you're someone we can trust," I fired back.

Jasher glanced toward the window, his eyes revealing the faintest hint of worry. Was he worried Trendon would shoot him? To be perfectly honest, I felt concerned with Trendon's handle on the machine gun. What if it accidentally went off?

"Trust is such an odd thing, isn't it?" Jasher asked. "It sometimes takes a lifetime to build, and yet a single event can dissolve it into nothing." He ran a hand over one of his sleeves, smoothing the creases.

What did he mean by that? Was he implying Dorothy had done something to break my trust? Wasn't that the same thing Joseph had tried to tell me last night?

"Aw, that's beautiful. Did you write that?" Trendon's finger grazed the trigger.

"No." Jasher shook his head. "I'm just saying you may be putting your trust in the wrong people. Take Dorothy, for example. She has earned your trust over the years, but I think you'll discover she's not what she seems to be."

"Let's just move toward the back, please," I said as calmly as I could manage. I glanced down at the scores of cowering people. They were confused and scared, and at that moment, I felt completely disconnected from the real world. Things really couldn't be the same now I had become involved in Dorothy's secretive life. Trendon and Lisa backed with me toward the rear entrance, but

Jasher didn't move. Neither did his men. They stood there as if immobile, watching us escape.

"You're making a big mistake," he repeated, his voice rising with an irritating melody. "I'm offering my services to you freely. I know things Dorothy doesn't. Codes, numbers, coordinates . . . Unlike her, I can keep you safe, Amber, if you allow me."

What was he talking about? Once I felt the glass door on my back, I pushed it open, triggering a tiny bell rigged in the entryway to jingle as we stepped through. Only when we hit the sidewalk did Trendon finally lower the gun and erupt with laughter.

"Did that really just happen? Did I really just do that? I can't believe how awesome I was back there. I kicked their butts! Me!"

Lisa sobbed and blubbered something incoherent. Standing outside, away from Jasher, would not have been my first guessed results. Trendon should have been dead. "How did you do that?" I asked.

"Dunno." He shrugged. "I guess all those video games finally—Oh, you gotta be kidding me!" Something broke his concentration. We turned, and my knees nearly buckled at the sight of several pale-skinned Architects piling out of the Roller Restaurant across the street, headed right for us. "There's a freaking army of these idiots!"

"Run!" I shouted.

Trendon tossed the gun strap over his shoulder, and the three of us took off at full speed toward the road. Cars had pulled over, with their drivers viewing the scene in shock. There were at least ten guys with guns charging after us. Why were they pouring out of the Roller Restaurant?

"Point your gun at them!" Lisa screamed. "Shoot them!"

Trendon's chest heaved as he sucked wind. "I can barely run as it is!"

Up ahead a black limousine pulled in front of us with the passenger door opened. I jerked my head at Trendon, who made eye contact briefly, glared at the imposing limo, and tugged at his collar, heaving for air.

"Ah, I don't know. Why not?" he wheezed. I didn't hesitate, grabbing Lisa's hand and yanking her toward the open door. I swiveled and looked behind me as Jasher's men closed in on the limousine, their guns at their sides. I expected them to open fire at any minute, but they didn't. Instead, they slowed their advance and lowered their weapons. Some of them smiled. What was so humorous?

The limo lurched forward as Trendon reached over me to slam the door shut. The automatic locks dropped into place, and the vehicle picked up speed.

"I think we made a terrible mistake." I grabbed the handle, trying to wrench the door open as the divider window of the limo lowered and a pale-skinned Architect glared back at us. His voice made a choking sound, one that made my skin crawl, and he smiled sinisterly.

4

"Bad idea! Everyone out!" Trendon ordered, shoving me aside to yank at the door handle.

The driver choked out another incoherent sentence, producing a sound like a garbage disposal, and Lisa clamped her hands over her ears.

"Stop it, please!" she begged. "Make him stop!"

Trendon grabbed the gun, but before he could remove the strap from around his neck and aim it, the divider window crawled up, sealing off the enemy. Trendon pointed the gun at the window.

"Should I shoot?" he asked uncertainly.

"What if it's bulletproof?" I asked. I had no idea if limos really had bulletproof windows, but it seemed a likely feature in one of the Architect vehicles.

Trendon growled and then poked the end of the gun toward the door lock.

"Don't point that at me!" I shouted.

"I'm not! I'm gonna shoot the door!" he snapped.

"What if the bullet ricochets?" I slapped the gun away from me.

He growled again, shook a fist at the ceiling, and then lowered the gun, huffing like a little child.

"Why does he talk like that? What's wrong with him?" Lisa had yet to lower her hands from her ears, but she no longer pressed tightly against them. Her eyes had transformed into a globby mess of makeup and mascara.

Trees, buildings, and other vehicles raced by outside the limo's windows as the driver steered us into the industrial zone just outside of Camden. Smokestacks surrounded by wire fencing and electrical transformers towered over the limo as it zoomed along the frontage road. As we approached a factory, I could see gigantic logs of wood piled high next to a variety of dormant hauling vehicles, tractor-trailers, and bulldozers. The limo slowed as we neared the factory. Was this some sort of rendezvous point?

"Hey! Where are you taking us?" I demanded. I knew it would be fruitless to ask him any question about our whereabouts, knowing I wouldn't be able to understand him, but I couldn't help myself from pounding on the glass divider.

The window never lowered, so I pounded again.

"Uh . . ." Trendon started to speak, his voice quavering with alarm. I slammed so hard on the window the palm of my hand went numb with pain. "Amber?" Trendon's voice grew in volume.

"Is that car going to stop?" Lisa squealed.

I turned to see what was making them so excited just as a white van seemed to appear from out of nowhere, racing at a ridiculous speed, and barreled into the front of the limousine.

A white light flashed in front of my eyes followed by the sound of screeching metal and shattering glass. The limo exploded sideways, and the three of us, unsecured by our seat belts, collided into each other as it rolled out of control.

The world turned upside down. My knees raked the ceiling as glass from the window rained down on our heads. Trendon clung to the seat belt strap for dear life. Lisa was on the floor, shielding her head from the glass, with her knee wedged under the seat next to the mini fridge as an anchor. The car continued to roll over and over until it finally settled against a massive pile of freshly cut lumber.

Smoke poured through the broken windows, and orange flames danced across the hood. The radio switched on during the crash, probably on accident, and the sound of opera music coursed through the speakers.

The divider between the front and back seats had shattered, and the driver, pale skin now splotched with red, stared around the limo, wearing a blank expression. His airbag had deployed, and the white balloon pressed against his face.

"Lisa? Trendon? You guys all right?" I rubbed my temples with my palms, all the while watching the Architect struggle against his seat belt

Trendon groaned. "That sucked!" He reached for the door handle but stopped when he realized my side was pinned against the log pile.

"Lisa?" I repeated.

She whimpered and coughed but offered me a meager thumbs-up.

The sharp sound of a switchblade opening drew all our attention to the front as the Architect began to slice his way through the seat belt.

"We have to get out of this tin can." Trendon kicked the glass out from the window of the other door and began to crawl but stopped suddenly.

"Why are you stopping?" I asked, plowing face-first into his heels. Looking past him, I released a cry of surprise at the sight of someone standing in front of the busted car window. The man had an average height and build, dark brown skin, and a black moustache. He wore thick sunglasses and a tattered camouflage jacket.

"Temel?" I asked in shock.

"The one and only!" Temel Ridio said, offering us a wide smile and holstering his handgun momentarily to help us through the window. "Out we go," he said, whistling some unknown tune.

As Temel helped me through the opening, I glanced behind him at the crumpled heap of white metal a hundred yards away. The impact with the limousine had completely smashed the front of the van, and the windshield wiper blades danced back and forth across the shattered glass. Of course Temel had been the one driving the van. Dramatic explosions and anything involving speeding vehicles were right up his alley. Still buzzing from the accident, I stared at him in shock. Temel worked with Dorothy and had helped Trendon and I escape from Mr. Jasher's clutches in Istanbul. I thought back to the war zone he and his buddies had created on the lawn of Jasher's mansion.

"Where did you come from?" Trendon asked.

Temel didn't answer. Instead, he aimed his gun at the driver as the Architect's speech grew louder and more excited.

"Don't!" I reached for the gun. "No more killing!" It had to stop. We were kids, for crying out loud, and I was tired of seeing it.

"Out of the way, girl!" Temel ordered. Refusing to back down, I grabbed hold of the nozzle and forced Temel to point it away from the Architect.

Temel's eyes became wild and angry, but he relented, pulling back the gun. Without saying another word, he tugged the three of us forward, urging us as far away from the limo as possible. The driver freed himself as the flames grew in strength. His piercing green eyes smiled at me as he peered over the top of the vehicle, and a slur of foreign sounds rattled out of his mouth.

Temel merely patted his gun affectionately. "Be gone, buddy. Consider yourself lucky."

For a tense moment, the Architect looked ready to charge at Temel. Instead he mumbled something else, bowed his head slightly, and scampered away from the car.

The flames from the fire spread, and something wet glowed near the rear of the limo.

"Is that gasoline?" I grabbed Trendon's shoulders just as the fluid on the ground ignited and the car exploded.

5

The acrid smell of burning tires filled my nostrils. Batting away the thick black tendrils of smoke, I rolled over and slapped away the gravel stuck painfully to my knees. How did this always happen to us? Deadly explosions seemed to be becoming a regular occurrence in my life. I remembered the Architect, and my eyes darted past the limousine now engulfed in flames. There was no sign of him, just a billowing blackness pouring out from the vehicle. The flames danced across the shell of the limousine, licking the jagged edges of the shattered windshield like a feathery tongue. It didn't take but a few moments for them to spread over the toppled timbers of the log pile. Immense, almost unbearable heat surrounded us, conjuring up the memory of a blazing bonfire, only much, much worse.

"I can't believe this! I can't believe this!" Lisa sputtered. "We were just in there!" Streamers of frayed fabric clung to where her dress had torn just below her knees, and road rash tattooed her shins and ankles. It looked horrible, but she didn't seem to pay any attention to her injuries. I imagined her wondering why she ever agreed to meet with us before her date with Michael. The movie would barely be halfway over by now, with the only burning smell coming from the popcorn in her lap.

Trendon wheezed as he scrambled to his knees. He spun around to watch the fire and ran his fingers through his hair in disbelief. "Aw, man!" he exclaimed. "You," he started to speak as he turned to face Temel, but pungent smoke forced him to surrender to a fit of hoarse coughing. After a minute of clutching his throat, he pointed at Temel. "You can't go a day without blowing stuff up, can you?"

When Temel realized the three of us were staring at him, wondering what to do next, he quickly holstered his weapon. "Ah yeah, right. Hmm." He bent over and offered a hand to Lisa. In the process of gathering up the belongings of her purse, Lisa either didn't notice his helping gesture or just ignored it. Temel stayed in that position for a moment and then offered the hand to me, which I graciously took.

"You okay, buddy?" he asked Trendon. With the back of his hand, he brushed dirt and gravel off of Trendon's shirt.

"I'm fine. Don't!" Trendon dodged away. "Seriously!" he shouted as the rubber from two of the car's tires popped and splattered across the asphalt. "What the heck do we do now?"

The question appeared to register in Temel's mind as all polite acts of gentleman nature vanished and his body stiffened with purpose. "You're right. I'm sorry," he whispered. "They'll be coming soon. We need to get off the road."

"Who will be coming soon?" Lisa had finally collected her items and stood next to Trendon. "The police? Those men?"

Temel nodded quickly. "Yes, both." He then pointed with his lips toward the industrial buildings and warehouses up the road. "Follow me."

"No!" Lisa shouted. "I'm not going with you. I'm going to call Michael to pick me up." She reached into her battered purse and searched for her phone. After several seconds of looking, she shook a fist and growled. "They took it!" She had surrendered her phone to the men in the restaurant. Her eyes brightened as she looked at Trendon. "Give me your phone!"

"Hold on, sweetheart, I need to make a call first," Trendon said, inspecting his phone for scratches.

Lisa fell on him in a fit of rage. The action came so ferociously, it caught the three of us by surprise. Lisa effortlessly wrestled the phone free from Trendon's fingers after slugging him in the stomach.

Toppling over to one knee, Trendon gasped. "What . . . just happened?"

"She just kicked your butt." Temel chuckled.

In all my years of hanging out with Lisa, I had never seen her act like that. That punch could've floored Temel, and he seemed to be in excellent shape. Temel's laughter grew louder, but then he held up the end of his gun in a somewhat threatening manner at Lisa. "Now, Lisa?" he asked with an inquisitive tone as if unsure of her name. The weapon temporarily gained her attention. "Please put the phone down. No calls yet. We need to get to safety."

"Are you kidding? Please tell me you're kidding," she said, refusing to let go of Trendon's phone. Temel's eyes flashed dangerously. "Why should we listen to you?"

I finally found my voice and joined the heated conversation. "He's our friend, Lisa, and he just saved our lives. I think we should listen to him."

Temel nodded appreciatively and adjusted his sunglasses. "Thank you. Now, hand me that phone and follow me."

Crouching low, we crept along just off the road, hiding whenever we could behind dumpsters and parked delivery trucks. It was after eight on a Friday evening, and the area seemed deserted. Had it been any earlier, the road would've been crowded with curious onlookers after such a major car explosion. From behind us, the shrill blare of sirens arose in the distance. No doubt everything from police vehicles to ambulances were now scattered about the main strip of Burdette Street trying to make sense of the disaster at Papa B's Burgers. Had anyone been injured back there? I didn't want to think about it. If I stopped for even a minute to discuss it with my friends, the memory would sidetrack us completely. We needed to keep our focus on something else and keep moving. Someone was bound to see the fire of the scorched limousine and would call the police. They would ID the vehicle from the crime scene back on Burdette, and it wouldn't take the authorities long to make their way to our current location. If they could find us that easily, so could more Architects.

Another explosion, not as loud as the initial one but startling nonetheless, erupted from the blazing limousine. I clutched my chest and noticed for the first time the stickiness of blood just above my collarbone. Though I couldn't completely see because of the angle and the odd location on my shoulder, I made out a small shard of glass poking out from the collar of my shirt, lodged fairly deep within my skin.

"Oh my gosh, Amber! What happened?" Lisa gasped. "Is that glass?" Her excited voice gained the attention of Trendon and Temel.

"It must've been from when the windshield shattered." I moved toward the window of one of the buildings and leaned forward to get a better look. "I didn't even notice."

"Oh yuck!" Trendon groaned with disgust. "How deep is it?" His panicked look made me worry. I didn't answer but gently closed my fingers around the shard, wondering if I had it in me to pull it out. The odd sight of the glass almost caused me to laugh. It looked completely foreign, and I couldn't believe it had stuck in my skin. Maybe it was only near the surface. There wasn't much blood, just a dirty gob clinging to the glass like glue. Fingers trembling, I nudged the glass as I tried to wiggle it free.

"Aye, aye, aye!" Temel smacked my hand away from the glass and delicately peeled back the torn fabric of my shirt to examine my wound. Several moments passed in silence. I felt uncomfortable under his scrutinizing gaze as he breathed through his flaring nostrils. Would I need to go to a hospital? That was out of the question. We didn't have time for hospitals.

"It hurts, no?" he asked, raising a thin eyebrow above the dark lenses of his sunglasses.

I took a couple of quick breaths to test my senses. Though winded from the accident, I didn't feel any pain, just numbness and Temel's calloused fingers tickling my skin.

"No." I shook my head emphatically. "It doesn't hurt." How could I not be in pain with a piece of glass stuck inside me?

Temel's lips quivered as he ran his finger across his moustache. "It will, sweetie. Very soon. Here." Rummaging in one of the pockets of his camouflaged jacket, he pulled out a bulging package of grape flavored Big League Chew bubblegum and a small bottle of rubbing alcohol.

"What are you going to do with that?" Trendon asked, reaching for the gum.

Temel yanked it away. "Hey! Is not for you!" His sunglasses dropped forward on his nose as he scolded Trendon with narrowed eyes. He then handed me a wad of the gum and instructed me to chew it. I couldn't understand why this was necessary, but I didn't argue.

As police sirens grew louder in the distance, I chewed the gum. We were running out of time. They were getting close.

"Okay, spit," Temel said, sticking out his hand.

I flinched. Did he really want me to spit my nasty

gum out in his hand? Why would I do that? "I don't want to . . ." Before I could finish my sentence, Temel stuck two of his fingers into my mouth and fished out the wad of gum. Too surprised to say anything in response, I could only watch as he rolled the gum into a small ball and doused it with the bottle of rubbing alcohol. Once completely soaked with liquid, he carefully stuck the gum on my shoulder. I felt pressure as his fingers worked, molding the makeshift bandage over the glass and completely covering my wound. He stepped back, cocked his head to each side to appraise his work, and gave an approving nod. "There," he whispered.

"You're kidding, right?" Lisa leaned closer to examine Temel's handiwork. "That's so not sanitary!"

"What?" Temel looked offended. "Of course is sanitary! This will help against infection."

"And you just happen to carry Big League Chew and rubbing alcohol in your pocket?" Trendon asked. "What else you got in there, MacGyver?"

Temel patted Trendon on his face, leaving a streak of purple slime from the gum on one of his cheeks.

"Seriously?" Trendon groaned, wiping the stickiness from his face.

I turned and once more looked at my reflection in the window. "So where do we go now?" I pressed my finger against the gum bandage and winced as a dull pain throbbed in my chest. The shock of the accident and explosion had begun to wear off, and I feared Temel would be right about his statement. This was going to hurt very soon, and it would probably be unbearable.

6

A deafening sound erupted from Temel's hand as he fired his gun at the bay door beneath one of the covered warehouse docks. With a grunt, he yanked the locked chain free and heaved the corrugated metal door open.

"This is the one," he muttered.

Gridmans Quilts and Notions, a fabric warehouse just off the main industrial road, rose up next to the railroad tracks. I had no idea why he chose it as our hiding place, but I didn't care. I didn't want to walk anymore. I needed to sit down and to sleep. Was Temel's chewing gum causing the pain? Would I be better off removing it? My whole body shivered. The weather outside, though pleasantly in the low seventies, felt freezing cold.

"Amber, you're pale," Lisa said, draping her arms over my shoulders and squeezing me tight. This action instantly sent a surge of pain through my body. "I'm sorry! Did that hurt?"

Tears welled in my eyes as I fell against her, trying to sap some of her warmth. "It's okay."

"Here." Trendon pulled off his jacket and covered me with it. "It's not much, but . . . uh . . ."

"Thanks," I managed to say with a pained smile. I couldn't remember a time seeing Trendon so concerned. Well, I guess that wasn't exactly true. When we were close to drowning in enough muck and slime to fill an Olympic-sized swimming pool just a few months ago, Trendon had shown plenty of concern then.

"Sir, we need to get her to a hospital!" Lisa said to Temel. "She has a fever, and she needs some sort of anti-biotic, and stitches, and who knows what else since you put that gum on her shoulder."

Temel scrunched up his nose and placed the back of his hand against my forehead. After whispering something under his breath, he snapped his fingers. "Okay, kiddos, tut, tut, tut!" He nodded toward the opening and pointed his gun over our shoulders toward the end of the deserted road.

The little light remaining from the sunset created a small pocket of visibility just beyond the opening into the warehouse. Stacks of wooden pallets towered next to an idle forklift. As my eyes adjusted to the darkness, I saw gigantic aisles stretching for several hundred feet in the opposite direction and a processing office tucked behind the outline of a soft-glowing vending machine.

"In there?" Trendon protested.

"Yeah, in there," Temel answered, not looking away from the road.

"But that's a death trap. They'll corner us and smoke us out!" Trendon didn't budge.

"That won't happen. Don't argue, just go." I caught sight of Temel's toothy grin, but the tone of his voice suggested he wasn't opening it up for negotiation. Reluctantly, Trendon stumbled through, and Temel pulled the bay door closed behind us. After fumbling around in the darkness, he found a mop next to the office and wedged the handle through one of the chain links on the door. He then directed us over where the light from the vending machine made everyone's face glow with an eerie reddish hue.

"Okay, everyone listening?" Temel asked. "Good. They'll be here soon looking for us. We need to find a good hiding place. So think hard and start searching."

"This is quite possibly the dumbest idea ever," Trendon grumbled.

"Why dumb?" Temel folded his arms.

"Because instead of going to the police and telling them what happened, we're running from them. Why are we running? You're not supposed to do that! We need their help!"

Temel shook his head. "No, *that's* a dumb idea. If we go to the police, you'll be arrested and then they'll hold you at the station. Easy place to find you if you're one of them . . . those *Architects*."

"Are you trying to tell me the Architects would try to nab us at the police station?" Trendon asked.

"Yes," Temel answered slowly, his voice rising with emphasis.

"Why?" Lisa chimed in. "What do they want with us?"

Temel exhaled. "I don't know why, but I was told to make sure to keep you safe and keep you away from the police. Orders are orders."

"Who . . . who told you to do that?" I looked up from the floor and stared at Temel's beady black eyes.

"Who do you think?"

"Dorothy?" I asked.

"Bingo." Temel snapped his fingers.

"Oh, unbelievable!" Trendon groaned. "Look, could you just give me back my cell phone?"

Temel frowned. "Nope. Not yet. You'll call somebody. They'll track you down, and then . . ." Temel pounded his fist in his other hand.

"They'll beat us?" Lisa asked.

Temel shrugged. "I dunno about them, but I'll definitely knock you out if I get caught."

We spent almost two hours hiding with no sign of any unwanted guests. My fever had yet to cool, and my head spun. Unable to sleep, I felt delirious and weak. I couldn't stand the thick, suffocating darkness of the warehouse. We didn't have flashlights, and Trendon's phone screen gave off minimal light. Plus Temel kept wandering off on some sort of patrol and would only return to check my temperature. Lisa slept quietly somewhere behind me, curled up on one of the aisle shelves with several bolts of fabric stacked beneath her head as a pillow.

"Hey," I whispered to Trendon, "you awake?"

Even though it was nearly pitch black and my eye-sight blurry, I could make out Trendon's smirk.

"No," he yawned. "I'm asleep."

"I can't believe you did that back there," I said.

"Did what?"

"Attacked that guy. You tackled him and yanked the gun right out of his hand! I didn't know you could do that." I had been thinking a lot about the events at Papa B's Burgers. Trendon's bravery had probably saved our lives.

"He probably didn't expect a chubby kid to put up much of a fight."

"Well, I bet he thinks twice next time."

I could hear the soft sound of Trendon exhaling through his nose as he chuckled quietly.

"Thank you." I reached over and squeezed his hand.

Trendon stared at his phone and gnawed his lower lip. "How do you feel?"

"Terrible. I think it's infected." I gingerly touched the skin around the wound and winced with pain.

"Oh, no doubt about it. You need a tetanus shot and probably some penicillin. If I had my bag, I could take care of that." Trendon always carried around major medicines in his backpack. Thus was the life of an extreme hypochondriac.

"I just wonder what's going to happen next. This is all so crazy."

The distinct sound of shattering glass echoed out from some distant corner of the warehouse.

Trendon killed the light on his phone and quietly

stood. "What was that?" he whispered. He nudged Lisa with his foot. "Lisa!" he hissed. "Get up! Someone's coming." She didn't budge, and I watched as Trendon searched the aisle for some sort of weapon. He pried a board from an empty pallet and held it up, ready to swing at anything. "Can you move at all?" he asked me.

My heartbeat thudded in my ears as I wheezed. "I guess. I'll try." I attempted to stand, but I had absolutely no strength in my arms or legs. I could hear footsteps approaching and turned to look, but this action brought on a whole new level of pain in my shoulder. I moaned, making no attempt to keep my voice low.

Temel appeared at the end of the aisle, only he wasn't alone. I could make out the image of another individual walking briskly toward us.

"Oh dear, my poor Amber," a soft voice whispered close to my ear. I bristled at the sound of it, but not due to fear. "Nice choice of weaponry, Trendon. Way to think on the fly. Now, can you stop threatening to bludgeon me with it?"

"Sorry, Ms. H." Trendon said, and the board clattered on the floor.

"Dorothy?" I blinked, but the blurry images dancing in front of my eyes refused to disperse.

"Yes, yes," Dorothy said. "Rest now." I heard the sound of some sort of plastic case opening, and then Dorothy's hand grazed my arm. "Do you have any allergies?" I shook my head and then felt the tiny stick of a needle in my upper shoulder.

An hour later, I felt lucid enough to slowly sit up.

Trendon and Lisa sat cross-legged on the floor next to Dorothy and Temel discussing the events of the evening.

"We were sitting in a booth at Papa B's with about a hundred other people on a Friday night. We could've been anywhere. They knew the exact location and the time." Trendon's voice grew steadily louder, and Dorothy held up her finger to hush him.

"Maybe it was just a coincidence," Lisa reasoned. She fiddled with something on the ground. I squinted and realized it was a shattered piece of her hairbrush; another casualty of the car accident.

"Coincidence my eye!" Trendon retorted.

Dorothy shook her head. "No, it was no coincidence. They must've been tracking you for a few days now. And probably had tabs on your cell phone conversations. Speaking of which, you haven't made any phone calls have you?"

Temel jabbed a toothpick into his mouth and scratched his nose. "No, I don't let them."

"Trendon's been on that thing all night playing games. Could they have tracked that?" Lisa dropped the brush and sat forward.

Trendon held up his phone guiltily. "If those morons found a way to track someone by their game play, they're much smarter than I give them credit for."

"You should be fine," Dorothy assured them.

I groaned, announcing my movement, and the four of them turned to attend to me.

"You up for a hug?" Dorothy asked. I smiled and leaned in sideways, keeping my wounded shoulder out of reach, to embrace her. "Wow, I missed you." She patted my hand. "All of you."

"Even me?" Trendon asked.

"Of course!" Her eyes widened as if she couldn't believe he would even ask such an absurd question.

"Whatever," Trendon mumbled.

"Where have you been?" I asked. Finally there would be answers. I had wanted to know the particulars for quite some time, and here she was, the one who could offer them.

Dorothy patted my hand again. "Boy, where haven't I been? Let's see . . . Well, for starters I just flew in from Corsica, Spain."

"Why there?" Lisa asked.

Dorothy narrowed her eyes playfully. "Oh, just a vacation."

"You don't take vacations," Trendon said.

I wanted to enjoy this moment of lightheartedness, but I couldn't. We didn't have the luxury of playful banter. "Is it true? Does Kendell Jasher really have the Tebah Stick?" I braced myself for the answer, praying Joseph had been mistaken.

"I'm afraid so." Dorothy answered so flatly it caught me off guard, and it almost seemed as though she was passing it off as old news. Unimportant. My stomach churned uncomfortably.

"How did they get it?" Trendon pocketed his phone and gave Dorothy his full attention.

"Yeah, didn't you guys move it to a safe location?" Lisa added.

Dorothy hesitated. "They . . . took it," she said, gnawing on her lip. "The location wasn't safe enough, I guess."

"You guess?" Trendon blurted. "It didn't take long for them to steal it." Trendon didn't even attempt to sugarcoat his feelings. My frustrations weren't directed at Dorothy but someone severely messed up. We had risked our lives to protect the Tebah Stick, and just like that it had fallen into the hands of the very person we were fighting to keep it from. Dorothy appeared unwilling to elaborate. I had seen that face before. She was unsure if the information of her activity abroad fell into the category of "need to know" with her students.

"Come on, Ms. H. You're not gonna hold out on us now, are you?" Trendon looked at me, and I held his gaze for a minute. What was the point of her discretion? We knew about the Tebah Stick, and we knew they were moving it to a hiding place. We weren't official members of her society, but we had done more for the protection of the artifact than most.

"We had taken the artifact to Spain," she said after several moments' hesitation.

"And somehow they intercepted it? What did they do? Was it like a gunfight? Did you guys square off in battle?" Trendon asked.

"Not exactly." Dorothy skirted the answer, and one of her eyebrows twitched. "What happened in Spain is not important. And now is not the best time to discuss it. What's important is that you three are all right." She leaned closer and pulled back my shirt to examine the wound. "Mind if I take a look? Oh, Temel, you didn't use gum again, did you?"

"It's good, no?" While humming, Temel pulled the gum gently with his fingers. The glass moved freely, clinging to the sticky substance of the gum. I felt a pinch of pain, but then a feeling of relief swept over me. The glass was gone. Like a rotted tooth, it no longer infected my body.

"You're going to need a tetanus shot, and I'm afraid my medical kit is lacking in that department," Dorothy said as she fed a small wad of gauze into the hole where the glass had previously stuck.

I no longer cared about my injury. Why wasn't Dorothy or Temel freaking out about losing the Tebah Stick? Didn't they realize the magnitude of that loss? Now it was in Jasher's, or even worse, Mr. Baeloc's control! I watched her curiously as she made the final touches to my bandage. Maybe she didn't want to dwell on it because they had messed up so massively. I could respect that, but what about what Jasher had said to us at Papa B's? Dorothy's avoidance of our questions made me wonder if there wasn't an ounce of truth in his warning. Was she hiding something that we needed to know? I shook away the thought. This was Dorothy. She was not only my teacher but also a trusted friend.

"Temel, where's the nearest hospital from here?"

Temel removed his sunglasses and wiped the lenses against his jacket. "Five miles east. Not safe there, though. We should probably head south." He returned the glasses to his eyes. "I think there's one outside of Newbridge."

Dorothy nodded. "That will work. Though I don't think there's enough time to get you stitches, and you'll have a nasty scar."

"I don't need a hospital. I'm fine, I think."

"Yeah right," Trendon grumbled. "You'll lose your arm thanks to Temel's gum wad."

I tilted my head to one side, curling my lower lip, as I rotated my shoulder. A faint tinge of pain throbbed, beneath the bone. Regardless of the ointment and the medicine running through my blood, if I didn't get professional help, there was bound to be an infection.

"Trendon's right. We'll need a hospital. Just a quick jaunt in and out. A tetanus shot, a better dressing of the wound, and then we have to be off. Do you feel strong enough to move?" Dorothy probed further.

"How do we get out of here?" Trendon asked before I could answer.

With Temel's assistance, Dorothy helped me to my feet. She checked both aisles and then pointed to the rear of the warehouse. "I came in through a window back there, and I have a vehicle to transport us to a safer location. This place could become a death trap if we wait long enough."

"Ha!" Trendon exclaimed. "Did you hear that? A death trap. That's exactly what I said. I told you hiding out here was a bad idea." He playfully slugged Temel in the arm. A stupid gesture, if you asked me, considering Temel still held a gun in his hand.

Lisa stood but hesitated when we began to make our way to the back of the warehouse. "What if the

Architects are out there right now? What if they know you're in here and they're waiting by your car?"

Dorothy stopped and placed her hands on Lisa's shoulders. "I didn't come alone. We have a plan. We'll get out of here, I promise you."

We dropped down from the window onto the lid of a dumpster. Temel went first, scanning his gun in all directions, then Trendon, Lisa, and me, with Dorothy exiting last.

Immediately the sound of gunfire erupted from somewhere close by, and we quickly took cover beside the dumpster.

"They're shooting at us!" Trendon shouted.

Dorothy peered over the top of the dumpster. "Not at us. Not yet, at least."

"Then who?" Trendon asked. "Raccoons?"

"Four of my men are holed up in a large paper mill two blocks south of here. They're acting as the decoy, and so far it's working. They've barricaded themselves inside, and the Architects have it surrounded. Eventually they'll get in, and though I'm not too worried about the soldiers—they can handle themselves—once the Architects realize you're not in there, they'll spread out and find us."

More gunfire rang out. We heard the sound of breaking glass, shouting, and then the vehicles roaring to life. "Our cover's blown. Move!" Dorothy ordered.

Headlights lit up the night as a black Jetta ramped down the road toward us. The roar of the engine sent a shuddering wave through my heart, but my pulse almost stopped completely when Temel opened fire and peppered the windshield with bullets. The car swerved and crashed into the cab of a parked tractor-trailer. A sickening crunch of metal and breaking windows rang out. We didn't wait around to check if the drivers were still alive, continuing our pace until we reached Dorothy's Ford Explorer.

Within minutes, she pulled away from the warehouses and onto an empty side road. Trendon and I watched through the rear window, expecting at any moment to see more black cars racing after us, but none came. Lisa dropped to the floor in the back and sobbed into her hands. I couldn't catch my breath as my shoulder throbbed despite the heavy dosage of antibiotic.

Dorothy never spoke as she drove and rarely checked the rearview mirror. Finally, after it appeared we were completely clear of the danger, Temel turned and smiled halfheartedly. In his hand he held an opened package of grape Big League Chew.

"Care for some gum?"

I didn't answer and felt myself finally let go as I cried almost uncontrollably. Trendon's body shook equally as violent as mine, but he managed to snag a handful. He released a deep quivering sigh and jammed the stringy gum in his mouth.

An hour later, Dorothy pulled into the emergency parking lot of the Scarlet Grove Medical Center just outside of Newbridge, West Virginia.

7

The solid stone walls of Mt. Arayat, the Philippine mountain, crowded around me as I walked toward an unknown destination. The first question in my mind seemed obvious. How did I get there? The Philippines were thousands of miles away in the middle of the Pacific Ocean. Everything felt so clear and real: the sound of my footsteps on the stone floor, the continual drip of water coming from some unknown source, the damp, chilled air passing through the caverns. I pressed my hand against the wall and realized I wasn't actually in Mt. Arayat. I should've been touching petrified wood, but the stone felt different: smooth and wet and glistening with algae.

In my other hand, I carried the Tebah Stick, and it hummed with an almost electric energy as it gave off an unnatural glow. I searched for Trendon, remembering I had a companion at my side when I first searched for the artifact. He wasn't there, but I wasn't alone. One of the shadowy creatures that had guarded the Tebah Stick appeared along the path several yards ahead of me. Though it never turned or acknowledged my presence, I knew it could hear me walking.

When I opened my eyes from dreaming, for a moment I felt lost. This wasn't my bedroom. The sheets felt stiff and the pillow had little give, as though I was the first to lie on it in quite a while. I scanned the room and saw the outline of a lamp, a reclining chair in the corner, and the soft green lights of a digital clock reading 4:30. The small square from the window on the door jolted my memory.

Scarlet Grove Medical Center. I was still in the hospital.

Reaching under my gown, I felt the patch of material pressed against my wounded shoulder. The doctors had reopened the gash in order to pull out the tiny fragments of glass Temel's bubblegum bandage had failed to remove. I could remember taking some medication and then being led to the room to rest.

"Trendon?" I fumbled around the bed for some sort of remote to trigger the lights. "Dorothy?" No one answered. "Anyone?" My voice grew with agitation. Where were they? I sat up quickly and immediately wished I hadn't as the medication had left me groggy and disoriented.

A shadow passed in front of the square window, and I turned to see a face staring down at me. His pale skin seemed unnaturally radiant with the fluorescent light behind him, and the Architect's brilliant green eyes never blinked.

Was this like before when I thought my nightmare had ended only to find I hadn't quite woken up? The Architect's face hovered behind the glass, his eyes eager and curious, as he jiggled the doorknob. Immediately I kicked the sheets off my bed and dropped my feet to the floor. My eyes flashed around the room, finally resting on the bathroom door standing slightly ajar. Perhaps I could hide in there and somehow pin the door closed long enough that someone could rescue me. I readied myself to make a dash for the bathroom, but the Architect only watched me for a moment before ducking down from view.

"Help!" I screamed, finding my voice. Where was the stupid light switch? And where were my pants? I felt vulnerable without my clothes and only the sleek fabric gown draped around my body. "Someone please!" I found the remote resting on a shelf behind the bed and pressed the call button.

Trendon entered the room first. "What's up? Oh, oops!" He turned away and shielded his eyes. "Why are you naked?"

"I'm not naked, you idiot!" I snapped, snatching up the blanket and wrapping it over my shoulders.

"Then why are you wearing a curtain?" he asked.

"Where's Dorothy?" I had no time for arguing. Trendon stepped sideways and the rest of my friends entered.

"What's wrong?" Dorothy asked, forcing me back on the bed and covering me with the sheet. "You need to lie down."

"I saw one!" I nodded at the door, the image of the pale-skinned Architect still fresh in my memory.

"Saw what?" Trendon asked, peeking through his fingers.

"An Architect. He was right there looking at me! Close your eyes!" I ordered. Trendon obeyed and spun around to face the wall.

"Are you sure you saw one?" Lisa stepped away from the door, and Temel ducked out into the hallway. "You were probably just dreaming."

"I wasn't dreaming. He tried to open the door and then left." I felt wide awake and more than just slightly embarrassed without my clothes. "Where's my stuff?"

Dorothy tossed me my shirt and pants, and I changed under the cover of the sheets.

"Do you think they found us already?" I slipped my arms through the straps of my backpack and winced as a jolt of pain shot through my arm.

"Easy, Amber," Dorothy whispered. "You've had quite a night. You shouldn't be jumping around and getting all worked up."

"I'm telling you, I saw him. It wasn't a nurse or a doctor or some random patient. It was one of them. Maybe he was a spy. If anything, he'll be calling Baeloc and telling him where we are."

"Nothing out there, boss," Temel said as he reentered the room. He was followed by a nurse, who growled at the sight of everyone hovering around me.

"This is not what I would call allowing her to rest," the nurse said as she moved Trendon away from the bed. After fitting a blood pressure monitor around my arm and checking my temperature in my ear, the nurse jotted a few numbers on a clipboard.

"We probably need to get going," Dorothy told the nurse. "Is she okay to leave with us?"

After looking at my eyes for a moment, the nurse frowned at Temel apprehensively. "That's not my call. I'll get the doctor and we'll see." She marched out of the room.

"Okay, time to say good-bye," Temel whistled. "She's not going to call the doctor."

"She's not?" Lisa asked.

Dorothy steadied me with her hands and nodded at Temel. "There's an emergency stairwell down the hall-way that leads outside to the parking lot. If you're okay to walk, we'll take it slow. Everyone stay together."

"What are we doing now? Something illegal I bet?" Trendon asked. Even though I was now fully clothed, he still stared at the wall with his arms folded.

"The nurse will undoubtedly alert the authorities, if she hasn't already done so, and we can't risk any more delays." Dorothy led me to the door and peered out into the hallway. "And if Amber really did see an Architect, then it complicates the issue even more."

Dorothy checked us into a hotel just outside of Charleston, West Virginia. Trendon bunked with Temel, and Lisa and I shared our room with Dorothy. The air conditioner hummed and rattled, pouring cool air into the room, and I didn't even wait for the lights to go out before I collapsed on the bed fully clothed.

The delicious smell of pizza registered in my nose when I awoke at one o'clock in the afternoon. Trendon and Temel joined us for lunch, and we ate in silence. I could faintly recall my dream from the hospital. I had returned to the cave and was holding the Tebah Stick. It had all seemed so real, but I couldn't dwell on it. Not now, with all I had to process. Car explosions. Frightening games of hide and seek. The Architects. Once again I was traveling down a familiar road, but the thrill to find the artifact was gone.

The enemy had it.

Had they already won? Kendell Jasher had millions of dollars and an army of thugs at his disposal. Not to mention his creepy benefactor, Mr. Baeloc, who undoubtedly fueled him with whatever else he needed on his quest for global domination. What did we have? I guessed we could get more money if we needed it, but that would mean dipping into personal savings. Maybe Lisa could do that without drawing the attention of her wealthy parents, but mine kept my account on close surveillance. Not that I wasn't trustworthy. My mom was a corporate CPA, and my dad a stockbroker. They would notice a dip in my account and would start asking questions. That is, if they hadn't already heard the news from yesterday's attack.

After we each took showers, we changed into some new clothes Dorothy purchased at a strip mall nearby. Jeans and T-shirts were much to mine and Trendon's liking, but Lisa rolled her eyes as she stared at her reflection in the bathroom mirror.

"I guess its grunge from here on out," she muttered.

Trendon looked at his jeans and then mouthed the word "grunge" with a shocked look on his face. Lisa noticed and quickly backpedaled.

"Not that there's anything wrong with that," she said. "I just don't like blue jeans."

"Uh-huh, sure." Trendon's shoes sat overturned in the corner of the hotel room as he lay sprawled on the bed.

Outside, Dorothy and Temel engaged in conversation beyond the opaque blinds of the hotel window. "I'll be back," I said, snagging my backpack and approaching the door.

"You understand, right?" I heard her ask Temel through the thin barrier. "You have to protect her at all costs. If you have to make a decision, you save her first. You can't risk anything. "

"What about the others?" Temel asked.

I gripped the doorknob but waited before opening it.

"At all costs, Temel," Dorothy repeated in answer to Temel's question. "Amber can't fall into their hands."

My hand went slack. Why was she so concerned about me? I felt both flattered and bothered at the same time. Temel mentioned the others. Was he referring to Trendon and Lisa? If that were the case, why had Dorothy evaded his question? It certainly seemed as though, at the moment, she valued my life more than theirs. Opening the door, I caught her by surprise, and she spun around, ceasing her conversation.

"Hey there. All cleaned up?" she asked.

Temel lowered his sunglasses long enough to share a wink with me and then flicked a toothpick over the side of the balcony as he strolled away on patrol.

"I wanted to thank you," I said, hugging my backpack in my arms.

"You don't need to thank me, Amber. Any one of your teachers would've risked their lives to save you."

I smiled. "Maybe not Mr. Jefferson." Easily ninety years old, Mr. Jefferson hated anyone under the age of fifty. Why he chose to teach World History to private school teenagers always baffled my mind.

Dorothy shared a laugh and agreed. "Yes, perhaps not Mr. Jefferson."

"What I meant was, I wanted to thank you for the gift." I ran my finger along the backpack zipper but didn't immediately open it when Dorothy's expression changed into one of puzzlement. "My birthday gift?" I added, hoping to jog her memory.

"Birthday gift," she sighed. "That's right, it was your birthday recently. I apologize, Amber, but I completely forgot."

Was this yet another mysterious ploy to throw me off track? Dorothy loved to do that sort of thing. She loved to keep me guessing, but something about her eyes told me she was telling the truth.

"You didn't give me the books?" I probed further.

"What books?"

If she hadn't sent me the two leather-bound books, where had they come from? I quickly made up an answer. "Um, they were just history books. I thought they could've been from you, but now I think they were from my parents." Perhaps it was childish on my part to withhold information from her. But if she hadn't sent me the books, it made them all the more mysterious. And since they were in my mailbox, I felt it was a mystery I needed to solve on my own.

"I'll make it up to you," Dorothy said. "I promise. Once this whole thing blows over, I'll buy you a nice gift."

"You don't have to." I watched Temel weave his way through the parking lot below, checking under the cars and tipping his beret as a greeting to anyone passing by.

The door opened, and Trendon stepped out. "When are we leaving?"

Wearing a colorful scarf around her neck and a lace belt tied at her waist, Lisa had managed to transform her otherwise dull outfit of jeans and a T-shirt into something a bit more elegant. She followed after Trendon, also appearing ready to go.

"Had enough relaxation?" I asked. "I thought lying around watching television was your idea of a perfect day."

"There's nothing on the tube except for dumb ole football games and cooking shows," Trendon said.

"I'm glad you're eager to get going, but we've actually set up a meeting in town at the museum with a couple of our associates. The three of you should come along for this one," Dorothy said.

"Why do we have to come?" Trendon asked.

"It involves you," Dorothy answered. "All three of you."

"Awesome," Trendon said sarcastically. "Are these associates of yours anything like your buddy over there?" He nodded toward the parking lot, and we turned to see Temel temporarily facing off with a cat perched on Dorothy's SUV. Temel's hand drifted toward his holster, and for a second I worried he would shoot the feline. The cat appeared to grow bored as it dropped from the vehicle, and Temel brushed his hands together, glancing toward the balcony. Upon seeing us staring at him, he flinched and grinned sheepishly, swatting his hand at the departing cat as though he were joking.

Dorothy laughed. "Not to worry." She waved at Temel. "There's only one Temel in my organization."

Trendon leaned close to me and whispered, "Thank goodness."

8

The Lionel Sevic Arts and Science Museum had closed for the evening, but Dorothy didn't seem concerned. A security guard greeted us at the door and ushered us in while checking over our shoulders.

"Thank you, Foster." Dorothy handed the guard several rolled bills.

Foster thumbed through the bills and then pocketed the roll. "Just be out of here in an hour or I'll have no choice but to call it in. It's my job, you know. What's with the kids?" Foster glared at Trendon, who glared back defiantly. "If they mess with any of the exhibits, it will be my neck on the line."

"Why would we mess with the exhibits?" Trendon asked. "We're not four years old."

"How old are you?" Foster's eyes narrowed.

"Five," Trendon said, rubbing his hands together mischievously.

"Look, maybe this is a bad idea. I don't like this one, and a hundred bucks ain't worth my job." Foster started reaching for the cash, but Dorothy quickly squeezed his arm.

"Don't worry about them," she said soothingly. "We'll be out of here on time. You won't even know we're here."

Begrudgingly, the security guard stepped aside and motioned us through.

Dorothy and Temel led our group to the staff break room, and Trendon, Lisa, and I sat down on folding metal chairs while they left to wait outside for their associates.

After only a couple of minutes, Trendon grew anxious and excused himself in typical fashion. "I need to pee," he grunted, kicking back his chair so the metal feet raucously screeched across the tile floor.

"They're going to be back any minute. Can't you wait?" I asked.

Trendon smirked and headed for the exit. "If they really need to talk to me, they can join me in the bathroom."

I was sitting with my hands folded in my lap, gazing off in thought, when I realized Lisa had asked me a question. "I'm sorry, what?" I asked, blinking back into reality.

"What is this all about?" she whispered. She had gnawed the polish off one of her fingernails and had started in on another.

"How should I know?"

"Uh, because you're the teacher's pet—Dorothy's prized student." She made no attempt to hide her sarcasm. "Doesn't she tell you everything?"

"You've been with me the whole time, Lisa. We're both equally in the dark on this."

"Yeah, but you know something, and you're just like her. You like to keep secrets." Lisa noticed she had been destroying her recent manicure and growled with frustration.

Keeping secrets? If anything, I felt anti-secret. I hated the cloak and dagger operation and not knowing what lay in store. Dorothy's mysterious, tight-lipped discussions with Temel actually annoyed me.

"Why are you getting mad at me? It's not like I have anything to do with this!" I leaned forward, trying to get Lisa to look at me.

She did, but her eyes reddened with anger. "Oh no? You have nothing to do with it? It's because of you I'm here and not enjoying the weekend. I should have never come with you to the restaurant."

"I . . . I . . . didn't . . ." I took a breath, held it, and released it slowly. "Is it my fault Jasher sent those men to Papa B's?"

"Maybe," she said, though her eyes softened.

"Really? You really think I wanted this to happen? Getting chased and shot at and nearly killed is not what I call a fun weekend. I'm sorry you're forced to be here, but I'm glad you are. I need my friends right now." I didn't think it was fair Lisa blamed everything on me, but what caused me the greatest frustration was the fact I knew she may be right.

I meddled. I always meddled. Even before I enrolled in Dorothy's class years ago and developed my love of

discovery and archaeology, I had been known as a med-
dler in my neighborhood. My cousins . . . my friends . . .
random people I hardly knew. They all cringed when
a problem arose and I happened to be nearby to hear
about it. I would voluntarily enlist my services to solve
the issue, even when no one wanted me to. Digging up
answers didn't always make everyone happy. Now Lisa
hated me because of my meddling.

The metal door opened with a bang, and we both
looked up, expecting to see Dorothy and Temel entering.
Instead, Trendon returned and had apparently found the
snack machines.

"They have Gushers in the machines!" he barked
boisterously. "Remember those? Mmm." He crammed a
handful of candy in his mouth and opened a can of soda.
The liquid bubbled up, and he quickly covered the opening with his mouth, sucking it down before it could spill.
Stowed beneath his armpits were several other packages
of treats he had purchased from the machine, and he
held them out like a game show model. "Pop Rocks.
Fun Dip. Zingers!" His mouth widened in awe as he
listed his treasures. "It's like this place is stuck in the past.
Awesome!" He tossed a package of Fun Dip to me, but I
made no attempt to catch it. The candy skittered across
the floor, and Trendon gasped. "Well, don't just let it
fall!" He hurried over and carefully picked the candy off
the ground, inspecting the wrapper for damage. "Aren't
you hungry? What's gotten into you guys?" His voice
grew somewhat serious as he apparently noticed the icy
tension between Lisa and me.

"Nothing," Lisa said. "I'll take some Pop Rocks." She held out her hand, and Trendon grudgingly passed her the package. It was his only one.

"You guys fighting?" He dropped into his chair and guzzled his soda.

I glanced at Lisa, but she ignored me, chewing on the candy in silence. "No, we're not fighting. We were just . . ." The door opened again. I looked up and felt my jaw slacken. Joseph walked into the room, followed by a bald, pale-skinned man with dark, sunken eyes.

"Joseph?" I leapt from my chair, as did Trendon, who spilled soda all over his shirt in the process. Lisa slowly rose, but when she saw Joseph's companion, she faltered.

"What's he doing here?" Her voice rose anxiously.

Up to that point, I had seen only a few Qedet at a close distance. Though they all owned similar features—pale skin, green eyes—they also had their own unique characteristics. Baeloc's facial features would be impossible to forget, but I could also distinctly see the differences in the face of the limo driver. The Architect standing next to Joseph resembled Baeloc, but he possessed discrete differences as well. And I had seen him before.

"You were in the hospital!" I pointed a condemning finger at the Architect. "I saw you!"

"Easy, easy." Joseph calmly motioned for us to sit. "This is Sherez. He's a friend."

"Yeah, to you," Trendon said, holding his soda out like a baseball. "We ain't buddies."

"Calm down. Let me explain. It was Sherez you saw

in the hospital, but I was there too. We were there looking out for you."

"Whatever, loser!" Trendon shouted. "Take another step, and I'll douse you!"

"Where are Dorothy and Temel?" I retreated a few steps until the backs of my legs grazed the chair.

"Right here." Dorothy appeared in the doorway.

"Yo!" Temel followed closely behind.

"What's going on?" Trendon asked. If he felt wary of the situation, he had a funny way of showing it. He busied himself by lapping up the soda soaking into his shirt and then biting into one of the Zingers from the wrapper.

"Joseph and Sherez have risked their lives to get here. Neither Jasher nor Mr. Baeloc knows they're here, so they don't have much time. But they have some information that could be helpful." Dorothy unfolded a few more chairs for the new guests, and we all sat in a circle.

"How are you?" Joseph looked at me, his eyes revealing concern.

"I've been better," Trendon answered. I didn't think Joseph was necessarily asking him the question, but Trendon's answer definitely spoke for all of us.

Joseph grinned. "I never got the chance to thank you for saving my life back at the mansion."

"Thank Amber," Trendon grunted. "I wasn't going to stop."

Joseph's smile weakened. Yes, it was rude for Trendon to say it, but he hated Joseph, and I did too at one time. But now, I didn't know how I felt. I nervously glanced at

Sherez and felt my spine tingle. The man staring at me with gleaming, unblinking eyes reminded me of Baeloc.

"Why don't you tell them what you told me?" Dorothy said, leaning forward and resting her elbows on her knees.

Joseph nodded. "Right. By now you should believe me when I say my uncle and Mr. Baeloc have the Tebah Stick."

"How?" Trendon blurted out. "No one's told us how that happened."

"They took it. To be honest, I thought for sure they'd never get their hands on it again, but I guess something went wrong. That's beside the point. They have the artifact, and they intend to use it."

"What does it even do? Control animals? That's not so bad, is it?" Lisa wouldn't make eye contact with anyone in the room.

"Yeah, are there going to be tons of zoo outbreaks? Whoop de doo. We could live with that," Trendon added.

"You're not thinking big enough," I said. "What would happen if our nation's livestock up and moved? Control the Tebah Stick, and you could control the world's main source of food."

"Yeah right." Trendon brushed away my comment with a swat of his hand. "That's ridiculous. Are we going to start seeing a bunch of cows migrating to South America?" He laughed at his own comment. Temel smiled too and pointed approvingly at Trendon.

"Be serious, Trendon. You know how dangerous it is," I said.

Trendon's laughing petered out, and he wiped the sugar from his hands. "All I know is you held the stick for quite a while, and I didn't notice any unusual animals hanging around. No bats or monkeys or whatever else you can find in the Philippines."

"What about those creatures guarding the cave? I controlled them."

"Amber's right to an extent," Dorothy cut off the argument. "There's a possibility Kendell could use the artifact in that manner, but that's not likely the route he'll take."

I couldn't tell if Sherez was smiling or not, but his expression never changed as he produced a small pad of paper and a pencil from his jacket pocket. He scribbled for a few moments on the paper, erasing occasionally, while we waited for his response.

Joseph took the message from him and read.

Mr. Baeloc will not be harnessing the Tebah Stick's power to relocate animals.

When Joseph finished reading, Sherez smiled. His teeth were yellow and disgusting. Perhaps he found it funny how we had all focused in on the animals. It did sound funny, but what were we to think? I didn't know there were other options when using the artifact.

"Don't get cute," Temel said, tossing a toothpick on the floor in agitation. "What does it do?" Maybe Temel realized the gravity of danger resting with our unexpected guests. I couldn't help but appreciate his edginess. Someone needed to stay ready for anything.

Sherez wrote in a similar manner to Mr. Baeloc:

flowing fingers, dancing across the page with almost choreographed movements. His message consumed several sheets of the small pad of paper.

Unlike before when Noah first held the Tebah Stick, the artifact will no longer bend the will of any animal. The design has changed, as has the purpose of the artifact. It can no longer be used in the same manner. Now, only the creatures from the cave of Mt. Arayat are linked to the artifact, and only the owner of the Tebah Stick can control them now.

"Owner?" I said. "You mean they'll do whatever Mr. Baeloc orders?" I remembered the sheer power of those creatures. Their speed. Their strength. I needed to but think my command and they instantly obeyed. Malcolm and the other members of Mr. Baeloc's team, though trained killers, were no match for the monsters while under my control. What would Baeloc have them do?

"No, he can't use it," Joseph chimed in. "I saw him try just before we left. It didn't work."

"You mean they didn't know how to use it," Lisa corrected.

"It's more than just that. They held it, pointed it, made all sorts of commands, but nothing happened." Joseph looked at me.

"Well, that's a great thing then, isn't it?" I felt a momentary sense of triumph. Their inability to use the Tebah Stick might only be temporary, but maybe it bought us some time.

"Yes . . . and no." Dorothy paused, her lips hanging on the word "no" for an extra second. "The fact they haven't been able to carry out their plans is definitely a win, but it just proves what we already thought we knew."

"And that is?" Trendon asked.

"None of them are the owner of the Tebah Stick." Dorothy's nose twitched as she focused in on me. "Amber *is*."

All eyes of the room turned on me. I didn't like the attention, particularly from Sherez, who still wore his eerie expression. "Me?" I gasped and then laughed. "How am I the owner?"

"Somehow you've become linked with the Tebah Stick. When you held it and controlled it." Dorothy pressed her fingertips together next to her lips. "Some artifacts have been known to do that."

"That's crazy!"

But it wasn't crazy, and I knew it. The Tebah Stick's power drew to me. I felt empty and alone without it. I remembered the constant dreams . . . nightmares I had almost every night. Were the monsters following me because of my connection with the Tebah Stick?

The sound of rattling plastic broke the silence as Trendon removed yet another sugary treat from its wrapper. "So does that mean Amber's the only one who can control the stick?" He chomped as he spoke with his mouth full.

Dorothy nodded. "We think so. And that's why Jasher has been trying to capture you. The fact he went to the school proves that you're not safe here anymore. Whatever they plan to do with the Tebah Stick, they can't accomplish their goals without you."

Sherez handed his next note to Joseph.

My master never had intention of using the artifact for its known ability. That wouldn't accomplish his main objective. He is searching for all three Weapons of Might. The Tebah Stick is the first, but it is not the most powerful.

I glanced at Dorothy. For a moment our eyes met, but then she looked away and seemed to be having a silent conversation with Temel. Regardless of what it could and couldn't do, Jasher and Baeloc were planning on using the Tebah Stick with other dangerous artifacts, which they couldn't do without me.

"Did you know about this?" Lisa asked Dorothy.

She closed her eyes for a while. "Yes, we've believed for quite some time there was a link between the Tebah Stick and the Weapons of Might."

"What are they?" Lisa looked at Temel, who could only gesture to Dorothy for a response.

"According to legend, the three Weapons of Might can be pieced together as one artifact," she answered.

"Like a puzzle?" Trendon glanced around the room at each of us before wadding up his last wrapper. "You gonna tell us what this thing does or what?"

Dorothy sighed. "It's all speculation. No one knows for sure. Most archaeologists don't even believe in the existence of the Weapons of Might. Only in certain circles, our society being one of them, has the search continued for them, but—"

"What does it do?" Trendon demanded, interrupting her.

Sherez held out another message as he beamed from ear to ear.

The possessor of all three Weapons of Might can control the world's resources. Its governments. Its people. Every living thing will abide by their power.

"Come on!" Trendon chuckled. "You're kidding. He's kidding, right?" Dorothy pressed her fingertips together against her lips but didn't answer. "Oh, that's awesome! You mean to tell me those morons have a weapon that could end up ruling the world? And somehow you let them take it. What kind of archaeologist are you?" Dorothy's eyes flashed with anger. She looked ready to pounce on Trendon. He must've sensed the impending wrath and quickly backpedaled. "No offense, teach. I just thought—"

"Cool it, Trendon!" I turned to Sherez. "What about the other artifacts? What are they? Where did they come from?"

Tilting his head to the side, Sherez wrote his lengthy response.

The Source, the Fire, and the Wrath. That's what Baeloc called them. The Tebah Stick is The Source. Noah was the first to harness its power, and it is capable of locating the other two. The Fire belonged to Elijah and was passed on for a generation before vanishing from existence. That much we know. The Wrath is still a mystery.

"Mumbo jumbo," Trendon mumbled. His words ignited something within Sherez, and he barked a few sharp words in his native tongue.

Lisa covered her ears and clamped her eyes shut. "Please don't speak!" she begged. "I can't stand that!"

Sherez's eyes widened with excitement as he growled, but when he saw Lisa's reaction, I noticed a slight change come over him. Embarrassment. Sherez seemed almost ashamed as he nodded apologetically.

"So the Fire of Elijah?" I repeated. "What do we know about it?"

Unlike the Tebah Stick, Elijah's Fire was less extravagant. Elijah was said to carry a small item with him wherever he went. It would be insignificant and simple. A scepter, perhaps, or a small staff, but humble in design.

"So we're looking for another scepter?" I looked at Dorothy and saw her face had paled slightly. I hadn't noticed the change earlier, but now she looked sick.

"If the Tebah Stick can control animals, what does Elijah's Fire do?" Trendon asked.

"Do you not remember the story of Elijah?" Dorothy asked.

Trendon groaned. "Yeah, probably. Was it on an exam or something? Why don't you just refresh our memory?"

"Elijah was the prophet who called down fire from heaven. He burned up the priests of Baal when they offered sacrifice to their gods," I said.

"Fire from heaven? Seriously?" Trendon looked skeptical.

"According to legend, that is what the weapon can do," Dorothy said.

"Baeloc intends to fulfill his ancestor's legacy," Joseph said. "He already knows the location of the artifact and is preparing to set up a base around the burial site."

"What do you know, Joseph?" Dorothy asked. "Can you give us some sort of heading?"

"Not really. I haven't seen Baeloc in weeks. He moved out from my uncle's base and set up camp somewhere else. Other than his Architects, no one knows where it's at."

"Come on. You have to know something," she pressed.

"Well, it's not much, but I think the site is somewhere along the Orontes River."

"The Orontes River is over 150 miles long and stretches from Turkey to Syria!" Dorothy sounded both anxious and agitated. "What about your uncle? Is there a chance he's learned something? Can you remember any slip in a conversation with him?"

Joseph smiled weakly. "My uncle isn't saying much nowadays. He may have known something about the location, but he hasn't told me, and I don't think he will."

"Wait a minute," I interjected. Something didn't seem right. "You said 'burial site'? As in, Elijah's burial sight?" Joseph nodded. "But that's wrong. According to the Bible, Elijah didn't die. He was taken up in a whirlwind of fire." I could remember that much from some Sunday School lesson. "Why would there be a burial plot?"

Joseph looked genuinely confused. "Um, I think you're mistaking him for someone else." He glanced at Sherez for confirmation, but the Architect's eyes only twinkled as he wrote another message.

Very good, Joseph read. *It is not Elijah's burial site. The prophet had a companion who carried on his work when he was taken up to heaven. That man's name was Elisha, and he was said to be buried somewhere near Damascus. Baeloc believes that before Elijah was taken into heaven, he passed on the weapon to Elisha.*

"Wait a minute. There's another guy with the same name? Elisha?" Trendon asked. "Couldn't they just be the same guy with a different spelling?"

Dorothy smiled for the first time since the arrival of Joseph and Sherez. "No, Sherez is right. They're different. So that would mean there's a possibility the location is in Damascus." She appeared dazed, possibly in a state of disbelief, and must've been feeling the weight of losing the artifact.

"So, boss, what's the plan?" Temel asked.

"Get on the radio and contact Abelish," Dorothy said. "Tell him we won't be back until we can secure the kids."

Temel nodded and stepped out of the room. "I know you just came from Syria, Joseph, but I kind of feel you should get back before someone finds out you're missing."

"Yeah, about that." Joseph bit one of his fingernails. "We can't go back. I'm pretty sure our cover is blown."

"Why do you say that?" I asked.

He dug his cell phone out of his pocket and brought up a text message. "About an hour ago, my uncle sent me this." He handed the phone to Dorothy. After she read it, she turned the screen so we could read.

I'd like to have tea with you when I return. See you in a few hours.

"It's impossible for us to get back to Syria before my uncle, and there's no way he'll buy any story I try to make up."

"That's fine." Dorothy nodded. "You two will stay with us."

Joseph's eyes flashed toward mine, and I immediately

looked away. I wanted so badly to be close to him again, but I knew Trendon hated his guts. After a few minutes, Temel stepped back into the room.

"Okay, boss. Abelish has been informed. But there's a problem with our hotel."

"I thought there might be," Dorothy said.

"What's wrong with the Cozy Inn?" Trendon asked. "No clean sheets?"

"Not so cozy anymore." Temel gave an awkward wink. "I checked in with the receptionist, and the place is crawling with Baeloc's men. They found us fast."

"Right." Dorothy rubbed her hands together. "We need to be on the move constantly. We're not safe here, and we need to be near an airport. Everyone listen closely. This whole area is about to get really crowded. Jasher has gained access to cell towers and all other sorts of electronic communication, so stay off your phones. We'll try to find a spot to rest tonight."

Joseph crossed the room and reached for my hand. Part of me wanted to react by yanking it away, but the other part of me, the part that wanted Joseph back as a friend in my life, gave in. His hand felt warm, kind of sweaty, which relaxed me more because I knew he was nervous.

"I tried to warn you, didn't I?" he said, but not in an I-told-you-so sort of way.

"Yes, I guess you did. That was pretty dangerous coming here."

"Yeah, well, I had to look out for you." Joseph smiled.

Trendon made a gagging sound. "Are you done with the barf talk?"

Trendon's words snapped me back into reality. I wanted to know what had happened to Joseph after we left him in Istanbul. He had direct contact with Jasher and Baeloc. He knew they had captured the Tebah Stick and had tried to use it. What other answers did he have? Hopefully there would be a chance to ask him. But now wasn't the right time. After gathering our things and checking to see the coast was clear, we packed into Dorothy's SUV and headed south.

9

After stopping at a sporting goods store to purchase several small tents, Dorothy drove until we crossed over the Virginia border and parked at a camping ground just outside of Florence, South Carolina. She paid for everything with cash. Gas, food, camping supplies. The money seemed to come from an endless supply in the glove compartment. Surely she hadn't earned that sort of money from her teacher's salary.

Shortly after setting up our individual tents, Trendon, Lisa, and I surrendered to our exhaustion. I had no idea how Trendon and Lisa were fairing, but trying to clear my mind to find sleep bordered the impossible. Lying in my sleeping bag, listening to the crunch of footsteps and the humming as Temel made the rounds through the campground, I wondered if somewhere close by Jasher and Baeloc's men were waiting to ambush us.

"Forget it!" I whispered, flipping on my flashlight and pulling one of the mysterious books from my backpack. I might as well be reading. I sifted through the pages for a moment and then opted to start at the beginning.

At some point during the early hours of morning, and after I had read every chapter of both books, I finally began to nod off. So many marvelous things happened in the Old Testament. Elijah had raised a child from the dead and called down fire from heaven on multiple occasions. But there was also his companion who bore a similar name. Elisha took over when Elijah was taken up to heaven in a whirlwind of fire. He parted water and walked on dry land, caused an ax to float to the top of a river, and by his command, bears attacked his enemies. How could they do those things? I began to wonder why we didn't see similar miracles happening around us, but then I remembered the Tebah Stick and realized I had already seen them.

"Amber?" Joseph's quiet voice roused me from half-sleeping. I sat up, knocking the book onto the ground. I could see the outline of his shadow crouching near my tent door, but I didn't answer at first. "Are you awake?"

"Maybe," I answered.

"Can you come out?"

"I'm pretty tired." That was true. I was beyond worn out. And how did he know I would still be awake at this hour in the morning?

"We need to talk," Joseph said.

I considered my options. Staying in my sleeping bag and ignoring the temptation to follow Joseph would be the safest choice. He'd have no power to mess with my mind. On the other hand, I'd never be able to sleep until I heard what he had to say.

Unzipping the tent, I found Joseph cautiously checking over his shoulder. With the shadows cast across his face from the moonlight, he appeared different, almost sinister. I found myself second-guessing my decision. I looked toward Trendon's and Lisa's tents and saw the blue-gray domes resting still in the darkness.

"What's this about?" I asked, lingering in the doorway. Joseph reached his hand to grab mine, but I withdrew it from him. "Just tell me. I don't want to . . ."

"Not here," he whispered. "Not out here in the open. We need to talk in private."

I clung to the inside cover of my sleeping bag but leaned forward enough to scan the campground. "Where's Dorothy?"

Joseph nodded toward her tent. "She's in there, sleeping." The window flaps had been rolled back, allowing the fresh, chilled air to flow in on her.

"How about Temel?"

"Gone on a walk, I think. Come on, Amber, hurry up." Joseph had his hands crammed in his pockets and continually shot looks over his shoulder with every disturbing sound.

"Why do we have to go somewhere else?" I retreated a step into the tent.

"It's okay. Just trust me."

Trust him? Could I do that? I didn't think I could completely. Not without learning more of what steered his intentions. I began to zip up the tent door to end the conversation. "I don't think it's a good idea. Let's talk tomorrow."

"No, Amber!" Joseph's voice rose as he shot his hand out, preventing me from closing it. "This can't wait." He puffed out his cheeks and slowly removed his hand from the opening. "Look, I know you think I'm all bad, but I'm not. And even if I was, there's no way I'd try anything with Temel on patrol. I don't want to get shot, and neither does Sherez."

My shoulders tensed at just the mention of Sherez's name. "Does this involve him?"

Joseph hesitated before answering. "Yes, he's waiting for us, just outside of the campground. But we have to go now. There's not much time."

"Let's get Dorothy then," I suggested. "I'd feel better with her. Shouldn't she hear what Sherez has to say?"

"We can't get Dorothy because what we have to talk about deals with her."

My eyes narrowed, but then my curiosity took hold. I crawled out of the tent and silently followed him into the woods. We passed several other campgrounds, with smoldering campfires burned down to dying embers and tents occupied by slumbering tenants. I didn't know why I allowed him to lead me away from the safety of Dorothy, Temel, and the others, but there were already too many secrets being withheld in our group. Dorothy had trouble looking me in the eyes. She had something she refused to tell me, and if Joseph had the answers as to why, the risks were worth taking.

Standing solitary by the outhouses, Sherez looked almost like a statue. His pale skin and unyielding features might as well have been made of stone. The only things lifelike about him were his eyes, though they seemed alien and unnatural. Like glowing green orbs.

The smell wafting out from the small bathroom stalls stung my eyes as we drew near. Joseph covered his nose and mouth with his shirt collar and nodded to Sherez, who seemed unaffected by the potent stench.

"He thought it would be best if we spoke here," Joseph said.

"Here?" I asked. "Of all the places to have a meeting, why the bathrooms?"

"It gives us an alibi if Dorothy or Temel show up. We'll just tell them we had to go to the restroom."

I rubbed my arms, feeling the biting temperatures of the early morning along my skin. "All right, I'm here," I whispered. "What do you want?"

Sherez blinked slow and deliberate, the radiant color of his eyes snuffing out momentarily before flashing back to view. He handed Joseph a prewritten message.

"He wants me to tell you things aren't as they seem and that you need to extend your trust."

I gnawed on the inside of my lip. Lately, everyone tossed that word around. *Trust.* "I'm listening." I would hear them out, but I refused to make any rash commitments.

You're in real danger, Amber. It's far worse than what we said to Dorothy earlier at the museum. Baeloc has altered his plans for the Weapons of Might. His intentions no longer align with some of our wishes. Though his followers are many, there are a few of us who intend to defy him.

Joseph looked up from the note.

"I don't know what that means. What's he saying?" Another cryptic message? How was I supposed to understand it?

"It means Baeloc is out of control and Sherez and a few others want to stop him," Joseph clarified.

"Okay," my voice rose anxiously. "Don't we already know this? Dorothy's letting you guys come along with us, and she seems to believe you, so you don't have to convince me, I guess."

"Why do you think we're here, Amber?" Joseph asked. "Why do you think we came all this way to meet up with you guys?"

I sighed. "I suppose you're trying to do the right thing."

Joseph nodded. "When Sherez came to my uncle and told him Baeloc's true intentions, we knew it was time to leave, and we came to get you."

"Your uncle?" I blurted. "He's here?" I whirled around, searching for any signs of Kendell Jasher.

"He's not here. It's just us. But my Uncle Jasher was one of the few who rebelled against Baeloc."

I couldn't keep myself from laughing. "Oh, please! You can't trust Jasher! And if you think I'm going to believe he's changed, then this conversation is over!" I knew I shouldn't have left the safety of my tent. "Your uncle is a wicked man. Maybe he's just Baeloc's puppet and he's been brainwashed, but that doesn't mean he's—"

"He's dead, Amber," Joseph said solemnly.

My teeth sank into the edge of my lower lip, and instantly I could taste the blood. "Who's dead?"

"My uncle's dead. Baeloc killed him, along with most of his men. "

"I just saw your uncle the other day, and he tried to kidnap me!" I backed away from them. Baeloc and Jasher were partners. Why would they go against each other? Suddenly I felt extremely exposed, as if at any moment enemies would surround me. I turned to leave, but Joseph caught my arm.

"He was trying to keep you away from the Architects, and Baeloc killed him shortly after."

"You weren't there!" I yanked free of his hand and hugged my arms tightly, trying to control my temper. Sherez maintained his silence throughout our argument, watching us with a sort of eager interest. "They had guns . . . and . . . and they were with Baeloc's men!" One of the Architects had been driving the limousine. How could he explain that?

"I *was* there, Amber. I was with my uncle up until Baeloc's goons caught up with us. Then I escaped. I just wasn't at the restaurant."

"What about what you told us at the museum? You said your uncle was heading home to meet with you."

"I did lie about that. I had to. I didn't want to tell Dorothy about my uncle."

"No, you're lying now!" I once again stepped away but then turned. "Your uncle's men shot up the Papa B's restaurant. They almost killed Trendon!"

"Think about it, Amber. What really happened?" Joseph's eyes narrowed. "My uncle's men came into the restaurant and tried to take you. Yeah, they're not the nicest guys, but if they were really there to hurt you, they would've shot Trendon and Lisa on sight. Yet somehow you all got away. One kid with a machine gun versus my dad's armed mercenaries, and you guys somehow escaped? Come on!"

Now that he put it that way, Trendon shouldn't have stood a chance against them. Why would Jasher just let us go? "But we got picked up by one of the Architects," I whispered.

"That wasn't supposed to happen. My uncle had tried to throw the Architects off your trail with false information."

I remembered the scores of pale-skinned Architects swarming out of the Roller Restaurant across the street from Papa B's. It was the wrong restaurant. Why hadn't they all been in the same location? At the time, I assumed they were scoping out all of the possibilities, but there were dozens of places where we could've been eating. Kendell had seemed to know exactly where we were, while the Architects had chosen incorrectly.

"You're lucky to be where you are right now. That Architect had specific instructions to take you straight to Baeloc."

The steady beat of my pulse countered the sound of my chattering teeth. The temperature had seemed to plummet, and I shivered uncontrollably.

"Why did your uncle rebel against Baeloc?" I asked.

"Uncle Jasher wasn't a good guy, but he didn't want the same thing as Baeloc. My uncle only wanted power."

"Only?" I raised an eyebrow.

"I know it sounds bad, but you have to trust me. My uncle had changed his ways."

"I'm sorry, but I don't think I can trust you. I want to, but . . ."

Joseph looked crushed. His shoulders slumped, and he averted his eyes from mine. "Look, I know you don't want to believe me, but if it makes you feel any better, we're not staying," he said.

"You're not?" Did that really make me feel better? "Where are you going?"

"We don't know yet, but you're not safe with us hanging around. Baeloc seems to always know where we are, and that would put you in danger."

"But you can't just leave. You won't stand a chance on your own. You're better off staying with us. Dorothy can keep all of us safe."

"That's the other thing I wanted to talk to you about," Joseph whispered. "There's something you should know about Dorothy. She's not telling you everything." This was the second time I had heard something along these lines. The first had come from Joseph's uncle. Apparently he had said these words right before Baeloc had killed him. "What do you know about what happened with the Tebah Stick?"

I felt a heavy lump form in my throat. "It was taken by Baeloc somewhere in Spain." Joseph nodded slowly, prompting me to continue. "It was an accident."

"That was no accident, Amber."

Both Temel and Dorothy appeared along the path, headed toward the outhouses. When they saw me, Temel drew his weapon and Dorothy quickened her steps.

"What are you doing out here?" she asked, starting to slow once she recognized me.

I turned to devise a quick reason, but Joseph and Sherez no longer stood behind me, having slipped behind the outhouses to hide. Dorothy and Temel hadn't noticed them, which made the situation even more intense. "I was just going to the . . ." I glared at Temel. "Um . . . you know." I nodded sideways to the outhouses. My pulse raced out of control. What did Joseph mean by that? If it wasn't an accident, then what was he saying happened?

"You shouldn't go alone, Amber. Next time, come wake me, and I'll go with you," Dorothy said.

I looked at her for a moment, and I knew she could sense my apprehension. Could I trust her? Was Joseph really telling the truth? It didn't feel like he was lying, but maybe he didn't know all of the facts.

"Is there something wrong?" Dorothy asked.

I hesitated to answer but then shook my head. "Nothing. I'm fine. I'm just . . . uh, freaked out, that's all."

"Let's get back to camp."

The three of us turned and walked toward our tents. I found myself occasionally checking behind us for signs of Joseph.

"What are you looking for?" Dorothy asked, eyeing me suspiciously.

My head snapped back in attention. "Nothing. I just thought I saw something."

"You okay?" she probed further.

"I'm fine," I lied. I was spiraling into a whirlwind of deception. If I didn't tell Dorothy about my conversation with Joseph and Sherez, it may as well be considered a lie. If I told her, however, she would try to convince me of Joseph's deception. I knew I shouldn't get caught up in the mess, but without knowing positively what to do, I wouldn't rat Joseph out just yet. Not until I had heard everything he had to say about Dorothy.

Unfortunately, that opportunity never came. When I awoke the next morning, Joseph and Sherez were gone.

10

Joseph's tent still stood with the door unzipped and most of the camping supplies Dorothy had purchased for him scattered inside. This could only mean he had left shortly after our conversation. A folded piece of paper had been pinned to my tent door, but Trendon got to it first.

"He says it's not safe for us to have him hanging around and that he'll try to contact you when he gets a chance," Trendon said.

"That was for me!" I slapped the paper out of Trendon's hand and reread the message. That was it? No more discussion? Obviously something had spooked the two of them to make them leave so abruptly, which made my suspicions concerning Dorothy grow in strength.

"Did Joseph give any indication of what they were going to do?" Dorothy asked once we had taken down our tents and piled back into the SUV.

"No, but . . ." I hesitated.

"What?" she said. "I know you two were talking by the outhouses last night."

"You knew? Why didn't you say anything?" I asked, trying to keep calm.

"What were you two talking about?" Trendon poked his head between us to join the discussion. "Did you guys make out?"

"No, we didn't make out!" I shouted, slugging him in the arm.

"What did he tell you?" Dorothy demanded.

I sighed and chose to come clean. "His Uncle Jasher is dead," I said. "Baeloc killed him."

Temel spun around from the driver seat. "What?"

Everyone echoed the question simultaneously.

"Apparently they didn't get along anymore and Jasher wanted to break away from him. That's why they came separately to Papa B's the other day." I glanced at Lisa and Trendon. "I never thought about it until last night, but if you remember, all of the Architects were in a different restaurant. It's because they were fighting against each other."

"Bull!" Trendon blurted, unconvinced. "Joseph's lying to you. Again."

"I don't think so. Not this time," I said. "It sounds like the truth."

"No offense, Amber, but I don't think you have a clue what the truth is anymore."

"Oh, and you do?" I asked defensively.

"Maybe not, but I'm not all lubby dubby with Jo Jo."

"Neither am I!"

"Guys, stop yelling," Lisa begged. "What else did he talk about?"

I thought about what Joseph had said about Dorothy. How the Tebah Stick hadn't fallen into the hands of Baeloc by accident. I glanced at Dorothy but decided not to share that part of our conversation. "Nothing. We didn't have time to talk about anything else. But it sounds like there may be others like Sherez who are willing to fight against Baeloc."

Temel put the vehicle in reverse, and we exited the campsite, pulling out onto the highway. Dorothy typed on her laptop and whispered continually in Temel's ear. Though I caught bits and pieces as we drove, I couldn't make out the bulk of the exchange. After driving for an hour, we once again pulled off the road.

"Okay, there's been a new development we need to discuss," Dorothy said, turning to face us in the back of the SUV. "Joseph and Sherez's departure have complicated things. It makes me nervous. He likely still has contact with Baeloc, which means we could be being followed."

"You think Joseph is a double-crosser . . . again?" Trendon asked.

"I'd like to think not, but we can't take any chances." For a second, her eyes rested on me and narrowed. Did she know what Joseph told me? If she did, why didn't she just confront me on it? Part of me wished it were already out in the open. At least then I wouldn't have this awful pain of guilt in my stomach. I wanted to keep my faith in Dorothy, but Joseph's words rattled everything. Maybe it hadn't been an accident. If that were true, I needed to know, what really did happen with the Tebah Stick?

"Then why are we stopping on the side of the road?" Trendon asked. "If we're being followed, we're not exactly making it difficult."

"That's what we need to talk about. Up ahead there's a freeway on-ramp, and we're about fifty or so miles from Athens International Airport. One of my closest colleagues will be there to help, but we need to go over the particulars."

"The particulars of what?" I asked.

"It gets somewhat tricky from here. We can't just go prancing into a public place acting suspicious. We need to stick together and keep low profiles. We'll need to change into some new clothes at the nearest rest stop and probably get something to eat."

"What are you talking about?" Trendon asked. "I'm not showering in some rest stop! And why do we have to go to an airport?"

"You have your passports, no?" Temel asked. He had stayed relatively quiet up until that point.

"Why would we have our passports?" Trendon raised his eyebrow.

Temel grinned. "Oh, that's right. Don't you fret, my friends. I took the liberty of bringing them for you."

Trendon looked at me, but before he could speak, Dorothy explained. "We're taking the three of you to our compound in Amman, Jordan. At this point, with the possibility of Baeloc's goons getting closer, leaving the country will be the safest for you, especially for Amber. We can't take the risk of her getting caught."

Several seconds passed as we processed the news, and

then Trendon exploded with laughter. "I'm not going anywhere. I'm calling my parents, and we're doing this the right way this time. No more spelunking in devil caves. I'm going to call the cops. It's been fun, but . . . well, no, not really."

"I'm with him," Lisa whispered. "I can't go to Jordan. I've been away from school long enough as it is."

Dorothy ran her fingers across her lips, seeming to debate her next choice of words.

"Listen, guys, I don't think you really understand what's at stake." She appeared apologetic. "Baeloc is after Amber, which means he'll be after you two as well. Your families won't be safe. You won't be safe at the school. Anywhere. Not until this issue is resolved. You have to come with us."

Lisa shook her head. "I'm not going with you."

Dorothy sighed. "We're not giving you a choice on this."

Lisa's eyelids fluttered. "No choice? Whatever. Once I call my father, I'll have plenty of choices."

"All of your parents are under our protection right now. Just until this blows over."

"WHAT?" we all shouted in unison.

"That's such a crock!" Trendon added. When Dorothy appeared serious, he yanked his phone out of his pocket and started dialing. "Hey!" he snapped after a second's pause. "There's no signal."

"I jammed it with this." Temel held up a small, black piece of electronics with a few blipping lights. Turning it over in his hand, he beamed at the object proudly.

Trendon scoffed. "And you don't think I can hack my way through?" His arrogant tone indicated his acceptance of the challenge. For Trendon, it would probably take less than a minute.

"No, we know you can, but we're going to ask you not to," Dorothy answered.

"Yeah, we say please don't," Temel added.

"Or what? You'll shoot me?" Trendon fired back.

"No, of course not." Temel looked hurt, balking at the absurdity of Trendon's accusation. "I'll just smash your phone." He smiled, but I didn't think he was joking and neither did Trendon.

"My parents?" Lisa asked. "They wouldn't just go with you. My dad's not easily persuaded."

"Once we explained the danger you were in, your father came along easily enough. Plus, our men are posing as federal agents, and they are very convincing," Dorothy added. "Don't you get it? Baeloc will kill you. All of you. We had no choice but to go to extreme measures to ensure their safety. Our actions are in your best interest."

"Where are they?" I asked. "Where are you holding them?" My hands were red and sweaty, and I wrung them together as though they were made of wet fabric.

Dorothy held out her hands in defense. "Holding them? Don't think of this as a prison sentence. Your parents are safe, and they're not staying in cages or cells. They have plenty of food and, most important, armed guards with instructions to protect them at all costs."

"What do our parents know?" My chest thudded anxiously.

"They know enough about the situation to understand how serious this is. And the danger the three of you face." She nodded to the road. "We need to leave now for the airport. We'll board a plane for Jordan, and then we can go over everything else."

"I want to talk to them," Lisa whispered.

"You will, we promise."

"NOW!" she demanded.

"Easy, easy, princess," Temel said, flicking a toothpick out the window. "You can't reach them just yet. You'll have to wait for . . . hey!" Temel glared at Trendon. "What are you doing?"

Trendon finished mashing a few combinations on his phone and smiled triumphantly. He held his phone up to his ear as the muted sound of dialing poured out of the receiver.

"How did you do that?" Temel looked baffled as he stared at the piece of electronics in his hand and then at Dorothy.

"That was fast, Trendon. We knew you could hack through, but please hang up that phone," Dorothy said. "You'll give away our position. You might as well send off a road flare!"

Trendon stared defiantly at the two of them for a moment and then glanced sideways at me.

"Just do it," I whispered. He shrugged and hung up the phone.

"So now that you know I'm awesome and that I can call out at any time, you better keep your promise. When can we talk to them?" Trendon asked.

"Very soon. Once we land in Jordan and we're in our secure compound, we'll make the call," Dorothy said.

I couldn't believe what was happening. It felt cold and heartless. Since when had Dorothy resorted to ultimatums? When she had been captured by Jasher and held in a Turkish fortress with no choice but to recruit us kids to come to her aide, she had given us options. Maybe that was because of her circumstances. Had she been free and armed with Temel at her side as a bodyguard, would she have used force to enlist us to the cause? I was beginning to believe she would.

11

Of all the things I had learned about Dorothy over the past several months, one truth stood out above the rest. Dorothy had connections everywhere. After a hushed conversation with a woman at the Athens International Airport, she escorted us through security, bypassing customs, and we boarded a small jet chartered for a transatlantic flight.

Small and thin, the plane had two short rows of seats, ten deep, with a curtain separating the seats in first class. Despite its size, Dorothy assured us the plane could easily make the distance across the ocean.

"That's comforting," Trendon grumbled as he plowed his way through to the back seats by the restroom.

Three other members of Dorothy's secret society boarded the plane with us. Asa and Gomez were of Latin descent and spoke very little English, if any. They were dressed in typical pilot attire and immediately took their positions in the sealed cabin. The third man wore long black robes, with the fabric covering almost every inch of his skin. Only his eyes and eyebrows could be seen beneath a black turban and facial covering, as he kept the neck of his robe pulled tight above his mouth. He had his hands covered with leather gloves as well. A sword hung at his side, and he wore a menacing scowl that softened when he shook hands with Dorothy.

"Guys, this is one of my closest friends. His name is Abelish."

"When will the beverage cart be passing through?" Trendon asked.

Abelish raised an eyebrow at Dorothy, who only winked in response.

"Trendon is not one to beat around the bush," she said.

"What would you like, kind sir?" Abelish bowed while keeping his eyes trained on Trendon.

"Soda. Chips. Pretzels. Peanuts. The whole gambit. If I'm being forced to fly across the ocean in this tin can, I want to eat until I throw up." Trendon plopped in his chair and kicked his shoes off in the aisle.

"We have ginger ale."

"That's it?" Trendon barked.

Abelish nodded. "We could try stopping for something on the way, but you'll have to parachute down. S'okay?"

Trendon disappeared behind the seat and groaned his frustration.

Before that year, I had never been out of the country other than to cross the border at Niagara Falls into Canada. Now India, Korea, and the Philippines all owned stamps in the fake passport Temel had given me in Istanbul. And after a few hours, when the private jet landed and taxied on the Jordan runway, I would have another.

I thumbed through the thick blue passport pages as the beautiful landscape of the Atlantic Ocean filled my passenger window. My fingers ran along the edge of the photo of an overly smiley girl with braces and curly hair from two years prior, staring back at me. It was my eighth-grade school ID photo. Temel must've lifted it from the Internet when he illegally manufactured the passports.

The plane entered a pocket of turbulence, and I instinctively grasped my glass of ginger ale resting on the tray table. Lisa sat next to me, staring at the various maps of a world atlas, a look of indifference etched in her facial features. We weren't quite on speaking terms, though we did share a brief conversation about our passports an hour earlier. She had smiled at my picture and had answered quietly when I asked about the various stamps in her passport—her real passport. Spain, Scotland, Australia, and Italy were just a few of her legitimate vacation spots. Her parents loved to travel, and Lisa always accompanied them.

Behind me, Trendon's sweat-socked feet poked into the tiny aisle of the plane. He could pretty much fall asleep anywhere, and despite the frequent pitching of the plane, he never moved.

"Okay, why so quiet?" Temel stuck his head above the seat in front of me and removed his sunglasses. "You mad? Not at me, I hope."

I wanted to glare at him or say something nasty, but I couldn't. Not with his goofy grin filling my line of sight. Temel insisted he worked on his own and took orders from no one, but I no longer believed that. He walked a slight step behind Dorothy and constantly waited for her decisions before he responded. Dorothy called the shots. Temel acted as only the muscle. Giving us no choice but to board the plane and lying to our parents had been all her idea.

Maybe she was right to force our parents into hiding. I truly believed Baeloc would go to any lengths to get his way, including harming our family members. But Dorothy had definitely changed.

"Why hasn't she come back to talk to us?" I asked.

Temel glanced over his shoulder toward the cockpit. "Don't know. I think she's talking to Abelish right now."

"About what?" I looked for movement beyond the small curtain separating the coach cabin from first class.

"Don't ask me. She's worried though." Temel sucked back on his teeth. "Something's not right."

"What's not right?" Lisa asked, catching me by surprise. "We're just going to fly to Jordan and hide out?" She laughed, and Temel could only blink in response. "Doesn't she think my dad's people will wonder where he went? Ask questions? Start looking? What about school?"

Lisa was right in all of it. My parents both worked. What would happen to their jobs? Could they really just disappear for a period of time with no consequences? Was the dean at Roland and Tesh so truly naïve, he would overlook another extended absence from three of his students? If we did indeed survive the whole ordeal, how could life ever go back to normal? I pictured Sierra walking the dorm hall, pausing by my door, and knocking. We didn't leave excused absent requests in the RA office. That could mean detention. My stomach quivered as I laughed inwardly. Detention? Was I really stressing about detention? I glanced at Lisa and was actually impressed by how calmly she seemed to be handling things. Her eyes looked cold and unwavering.

"Would you please keep it down?" Trendon grumbled from behind us. His foot twitched and then rolled to the side.

"How can you sleep right now?" I fired back. "All you've done is eat, sleep, and play on your phone! You're not helping."

Heavy breathing. A few soft snores. Trendon had fallen back under.

I sighed. "Look." I made eye contact with Temel to get his attention. "We need answers. We need to know what we're doing and what could happen."

Temel twirled a toothpick between his thumb and forefinger and shrugged. "She told you everything she knows."

"That's a lie." Lisa threw the atlas on the floor.

"She's right." Dorothy appeared in the aisle, looking exhausted. "We haven't told you everything, but we will now." She braced herself against the back of one of the seats as the plane pitched sideways momentarily. Joining Temel in front of us, she stared down over the cushion. "What do you want to know?"

"Okay, for starters, how long have you known that only I could use the Tebah Stick?"

Dorothy moistened her lips. "We had suspicions that could happen long before you ever came into the equation. The Tebah Stick is not the first to act in such a manner. Certain artifacts have been known to cling to the energy of the first person controlling it."

I thought back to the cave in the Philippines. To the statue of Noah standing in the center of the room, extending the artifact like a welcome gift. "But Trendon touched it too, maybe even before me." I couldn't remember exactly how it all happened. That part of my memory seemed distant and clouded.

"True, but you released it from the statue," Trendon said. "You harnessed its power to control those creatures. Don't you remember? After Jasher and Baeloc fled from the cave, there was a moment when you wanted to give me the artifact. We were still surrounded by those creatures, and I knew if I tried to use the artifact, there was a definite chance it wouldn't work. I wouldn't be able to control them, and I felt certain they would attack me. I knew then, almost without any hesitation, you were the only one who could keep them at bay."

"How could you do that to her?" Lisa asked. "You knew what would happen if she touched the artifact, and you didn't warn her at all. Didn't you think she should know?"

My throat tightened. Why hadn't I ever thought about it that way? Dorothy had put my life at risk without giving me all of the facts.

Dorothy nodded. "Looking back, I realized I made a mistake by not giving Amber and Trendon all of the particulars. But I honestly didn't believe they would make it as far as they did. It was my last chance to keep it out of the enemy's hands, so no, I didn't think about that bit of information."

Trendon sat up and leaned over the seat. "Wait a minute. Let me get this straight. You didn't think we would make it as far as we did? How far did you think we'd make it?"

"Does it matter?" Dorothy asked.

"Uh . . . yeah, because if you thought we'd end up dead long before we got to the Philippines, that kinda makes you a bad teacher." He yawned and smacked his lips as though hungry. "Snacks?"

Dorothy jabbed a thumb to where a small knapsack bulging with granola bars and crackers lay sideways in the seat across the aisle.

Trendon groaned. "Crackers? Dried oats? What are we, horses?" Despite his loud protesting, he crossed the aisle and dug out a few of the healthy snacks.

"Don't you understand by now what's at stake?" Dorothy ran her fingers through her hair. "These artifacts have incredible power. And if in the wrong hands, they could mean the destruction of nations. Sacrifices must be made to keep that from happening."

"Yeah, well, sacrifice yourself." Trendon bit into a granola bar, flaring his nostrils with annoyance.

"Who is Mr. Baeloc, really? Who are the Architects?" I asked. The chattering growls of Baeloc, Sherez, and the limo driver instantly flooded through my mind. They seemed like monsters. I imagined them as vampires circling around in the air with their pale skin and eerie green eyes. Why did they talk that way? It felt like more than just a speech impediment. Their voices were unnatural. Evil. What purpose did the Architects have, and why were they so determined to cause devastation?

"According to biblical lore, a tower built with the purpose of reaching heaven was constructed in the land of Shinar, or present-day Iraq. This happened some four thousand years ago, and from the Bible we learn the people were unsuccessful in their attempt because God punished them for trying. The tower was destroyed and their languages confounded, forcing them to scatter throughout the world."

"I remember the story," Trendon said. "But what does that have to do with Baeloc?"

Dorothy ducked down in her seat and returned holding a severely tattered leather book with yellowed pages and a number of ribbons and bookmarks protruding from the edge.

"This is the Book of Despar," she said. "These writings were discovered on papyrus scrolls inside a cave near Saudi Arabia. It contains a history of happenings at or around Shinar directly following the destruction of the Tower of Babel."

"I've never heard of that," I said, timidly reaching for the book when Dorothy offered it. The leather felt smooth and soft, and the pages crinkled as I carefully pulled open the cover.

"That's because it has never been included in the Hebrew Bible. We believe it's due to the content."

"What's in it?" Trendon leaned over my shoulder as I thumbed through the pages. Several passages had been highlighted or underlined in pencil. A few of the pages hid small scraps of paper containing scribbled Hebraic characters.

"The writings of Despar," Dorothy answered flatly. "The original architect of the Tower of Babel and Baeloc's oldest known ancestor."

My fingers faltered on one of the pages. A crudely drawn image of a man with a pointed beard and thick eyebrows stared up at me.

"Despar?" I asked, showing the drawing to Dorothy.

She nodded. "Yes, at least one artist's depiction of him."

In the image, Despar wore several pieces of gaudy jewelry: a thick-banded necklace, rings on most of his fingers, and bracelets.

"According to this book, Despar was known as the most brilliant and talented architect. There are drawings of some of his work near the back." She pointed, and I flipped over to see several buildings with domed ceilings and primitive scaffolding circling the structures. "He was loved by all and esteemed as a man destined for greatness. But that praise wasn't enough for him. In the book, he wrote of his desires to solidify his name as the greatest architect the world would ever know. Sometime around 2400 BC, work began on a great tower, with Despar serving as the primary architect. A tower capable, according to legend, of entering heaven. May I?" Dorothy asked. I handed her the book, and she opened it to a section she had previously bookmarked. "In chapter seventeen, Despar announces his promise of redemption. Supposedly, when the tower fell and God confounded the people's language, Despar suffered the greatest amount for his primary role in constructing the abomination. His family was shunned, and many were sought after and murdered. And their voices . . ." Dorothy centered a pair of reading glasses on the bridge of her nose. Finding her mark with a finger, she began to read,

". . . *became as the rumblings of beasts. Pain plagued our throats as we labored daily to adopt a new manner of speaking. But our curse was grievous to bear. We understood all yet were understood by none. Shunned by those who once sought our counsel, we were spat upon and stoned. We found no refuge in the lands of our inheritance and were driven out to scratch an existence. Yea, and ever we went, the voices followed and mocked and made for naught our means of comfort."*

She closed the book. "Despar and what was left of his family went into hiding and felt the world had mistreated him and should've overlooked his temporary lapse in judgment."

The plane careened into another pocket of turbulence, this one a particularly nasty one. My glass of ginger ale danced across the tray table before toppling to the floor, spilling the remaining ice and soda on the worn carpet.

"Is it stormy?" Temel shouted, peering out the window as the plane made a wicked pitch to the left.

Lisa collapsed into me, causing my face to smash against my own window. Outside, the air seemed calm and clear with no signs of storms.

The first-class curtain snapped open, and Abelish emerged with sword in hand. Something dark and wet glistened on the blade, and I swallowed air as I gasped at the sight of it.

"Aw man, I knew that dude was twisted!" Trendon shouted, springing to his feet.

"Abelish?" Dorothy also rose to her feet. She gestured to the front of the plane, and Abelish glanced over his shoulder.

"Where did you find those guys?" He dragged the blade across an empty seat to wipe the blood clean from the steel.

"They're members of the society. We should've been able to trust them." Dorothy's voice grew with panic.

"They were personal associates of Baeloc," Abelish said.

Dorothy groaned. "No!"

Abelish nodded his head.

"How do you know that?" I asked.

Abelish ignored my question and jabbed the point of his sword toward Temel. "You, Temel? You can fly this?"

Temel stood slowly, his hand resting on his holster. "Yeah, I think so. Why do I need to?"

"Because Baeloc's personal associates are dead now," Abelish muttered.

"*Dead?*" I gripped Lisa's elbow. "Why are the pilots dead?"

"I killed them." Abelish scratched his nose with a finger and sniffed. His mannerisms seemed so casual; he could've easily just woken from a long nap. Dorothy looked pale yet again, but before she could speak, Abelish continued. "I recognized one of the men, Asa, when I boarded. He's a traitor. He's sold many pieces of information to the likes of Baeloc and others. Plus," he said, looking knowingly at Dorothy, "I believe he was the getaway pilot for Emmanuel during the Spain debacle."

Dorothy looked defeated as she clasped a hand over her mouth. Who was this Emmanuel? I had never heard his name mentioned before. I wanted to pry to find out more about him, but it didn't feel like the proper moment.

"Gomez may have been okay, but I didn't take any chances. Wrong place, wrong time, you know?" Abelish chuckled. When no one shared in his bit of humor, his laughter died off. "Anyway, I heard Asa talking on the radio to some man in the Nevatim Airbase in Israel. He was going to land the plane there, and they were going to take all of us into custody. So I decided to take charge."

"How's the plane still flying straight?" Trendon's voice rose up from behind me.

Abelish glanced once again behind him toward the front of the plane and shrugged. "It is a mystery, for certain. That's why Temel, my friend, you need to, uh . . . chop, chop." He nodded his head vigorously as the plane, finally realizing it no longer had a pilot, began to dive. Temel moved into the aisle, cautiously sidestepped Abelish's nasty weapon, and disappeared past the curtain.

"What do we do now?" Trendon shouted. He grabbed my arm, and I screamed in surprise.

"I don't know! I've never been in a plane crash situation before. Lisa?" I turned to her, expecting to see a teary mess. Lisa, however, appeared to be in better control than the rest of us.

"My dad's a pilot and flies his own planes all the time. We need to prepare for a crash landing." She looked around at the three of us. "Everyone sit down and get buckled!"

"Oh right, cause that's really gonna help us when we skip across the ocean like a rock!" Despite his sarcastic complaining, Trendon sat down and strapped his seat belt across his lap. We all did, including Dorothy. Abelish charged to the front, snapping open the curtain to give us full view of the cabin. We watched as he assisted Temel in dragging the bodies of the recently deceased out of the cockpit and into the first-class aisle.

"I think I'm gonna—" Trendon began to mutter, but then I heard him retching in the seat behind me. He coughed, spat, and then laughed a little. "Yep, a lot of good those granola bars did."

My eyes closed, and my hands shook, but I started to laugh, and soon Lisa joined in. Perhaps it was the extreme danger we all faced coupled with Trendon's spot-on humor that caused us to laugh hysterically.

The plane bucked, and the windows rattled so loudly I half expected them to implode. Thin, wispy clouds raced past the circular opening at blinding speed.

"I need a new seat," Trendon groaned.

I laughed even louder. Lisa's hand closed around mine and squeezed. She continued to laugh right along with me. Had we lost our minds?

"Hey." Trendon's head poked up. "Be honest, Ms. H., Temel doesn't have a clue what he's doing, does he?" Dorothy didn't answer. "I'll take that as a no. So, if we crash in the ocean at this speed, we'll shatter into a million pieces. They'll never find our bodies."

"Please shut up, Trendon!" she said.

"He's right, though," Lisa said. "We're not going to make it."

For a fleeting moment, my heart sank and I wanted to throw up in the seat just like Trendon. But then I thought of something and giggled again. "Can you imagine the look on Baeloc's face when he realizes he'll never be able to use the Tebah Stick? He's gonna have a cow!" What was wrong with me? Why did I think any of this was funny?

The plane continued to rattle and jump but steadily leveled out. Outside the window, the ocean looked frighteningly close, but we no longer descended. Something crackled overhead, followed by static, and then Temel's accented voice poured out over the intercom.

"This is your captain speaking. Call me captain from now on and forever!" He spat out something in a foreign language and pounded the microphone with his hand. "Is this even working?"

12

Our plane landed without any other incident at the Queen Alia International Airport in Jordan later that afternoon. Getting off the plane without drawing the attention of the Jordanian police, however, proved to be a little tricky. Transporting dead bodies on a plane, which weren't dead at the beginning of the flight, registered as a pretty hefty crime in Jordan. Temel and Abelish covered the bodies with blankets from one of the overhead compartments and stashed them standing up in the small restroom. We then hurriedly climbed down to the tarmac, where Abelish had a dark green van with tinted windows waiting to transport us to Dorothy's compound.

At around six o'clock, Abelish drove the van into a covered parking garage next to an enormous shopping mall. After leaving the keys in the ignition, he tossed a small brown bundle into the backseat of the van.

"That's money," Trendon whispered. "I saw him counting it earlier."

"Why is he putting money in a bag in the back of the van?" Lisa asked.

"He's buying off the local authorities," Dorothy answered, standing behind us. "Abelish is one of the great thinkers of our organization. He's already thought out the next several steps to cover our tracks and keep us well hidden from Baeloc."

"How's putting money in the back going to cover our tracks?" Trendon shoved his hands in his pockets but kept his eyes on Abelish, always watching his movements.

"In one hour, two Jordanian police officers will enter the garage by way of the service elevator," Abelish said. Apparently, he overheard our conversation. "They will take the payoff and remove the van. They will then enter the security booth of the garage and destroy the surveillance footage currently shooting us as we speak. Two thousand dollars won't buy you much in America, but here, if paid to the right people, that money will erase any evidence completely. That includes security footage from the airport and any traffic cameras along the way to the garage."

I was sure we all still felt the rattling effects of nearly crashing to our deaths over the ocean, but Dorothy's behavior seemed different. She had not been the same since our meeting with Joseph and Sherez. Where was the teacher so willing to share all of her secrets with me? Yes, she enjoyed keeping me guessing, but she used to make the answers possible to achieve.

A gated guard post with four soldiers dressed in military fatigues and toting guns surrounded the entrance of Dorothy's compound. The compound was nothing more than several smaller buildings without windows and what looked to be a six- or seven-story hotel resting in the center. Razor wire twirled along the roof of the hotel, and more armed soldiers paced back and forth on the top floor. One of the guards at the outpost shone his flashlight in our faces as Abelish barked instructions to the others. We were then escorted through the lobby.

"Have a seat and make yourself comfortable," Dorothy said, pointing to several chairs seated next to the restrooms. "Abelish, Temel, and I will go into the city and bring you back a meal. We'll be back shortly, and we'll eat in the dining hall down there." She nodded past the restrooms to a closed door.

A long, wooden banquet table rested in the center of the dining room, with metal chairs for seats. The table had only one decoration: a copper bowl of overripe pears. Centered on the wall directly behind the table was an enormous world map with tiny pushpins in various colors dotting across the continents. The highest concentration of pins dotted the regions of Northern Africa and Southern Europe.

Lisa nodded toward the table, and the three of us sat down. After several silent moments, Trendon whistled nonchalantly and reached for a squishy pear from the bowl. I quickly swatted his hand with my fork.

"Hey, slappy!" Trendon shouted. He flung backward in his chair, almost overturning it, and rubbed his hand against his chest.

"Don't you think we should wait for the others?"

"Wait for what?" Trendon huffed and held up his hand to show me where the end of my fork had left a mark.

"I didn't mean to hit you so hard," I whispered.

"You never do." Trendon sulked. "And why are we waiting, anyway? Do you think they'll bring us menus or something? Maybe they'll have crayons to color the place mats." He rolled his eyes when the two of us didn't laugh.

"Trendon, there's a thing called manners," Lisa said, siding with me.

Trendon threw his hands up. "Anyway. What do you guys think about Abelish?"

"What about him?" Lisa asked.

"He's weird."

Though different, I didn't necessarily think of Abelish as weird. "He seems fine to me, although he does carry around a sword."

"Not just carries it around," Trendon pointed out. "He hacks people up with it. Who does that nowadays? Plus, it's like 75 degrees outside, and he's covered from head to toe in a toga."

"It's not a toga. That's just part of the culture," I said.

Lisa drummed her fingers on the table softly. "I don't think that's it. When we were on the plane, some of his robes pulled back on his wrists, and I noticed something on his skin."

"Blood?" Trendon asked.

Lisa shook her head. "No, some sort of rash or skin . . . problem. I think he has a condition."

Trendon's shoulders slumped. "A rash? Like what kind of rash?" He instinctively scratched his own wrists.

"I don't know. There were lumps. Big ones on his arms. I think he wears the robes to cover them."

I hadn't noticed Abelish's skin disorder, but it would explain not only the robe and the head covering but also the gloves.

"Yeesh!" Trendon shuddered and rubbed his hands on his jeans. "Did he touch anything with his skin that I might've touched?" Trendon had his own condition. He was a hypochondriac of the highest degree.

"Grow up!" I said as the door opened and Dorothy walked in carrying two grease-stained paper sacks. Abelish entered after her, hefting a heavy cooler sloshing with ice and cans of soda.

"Sorry about the wait," she said, placing the sacks on the table and peeling back the paper. "Takeout isn't easy to get here in Amman anymore, especially now that we're under constant watch. Luckily, Abelish's niece lives just a few miles south of here in Sahab, and she's quite the chef."

Trendon eyeballed the containers of food. "Niece? Do you guys live together?" he asked suspiciously.

Abelish slid the cooler on the floor and looked over at Trendon. "No. She has her own family."

"Does she wear . . . uh . . . robes and stuff like you too?" Trendon tried to act casual.

"What are you doing?" I asked under my breath.

Abelish opened a can of soda and leaned his head back to drink. Though carefully covered by his robes, I could faintly make out several strange splotches above his cheekbones. His skin seemed somewhat unnatural.

"You don't like what I wear?" Abelish wiped his mouth with his sleeve.

"No, no. It's awesome. I just . . . dang it!" he shouted after I kicked him squarely in the shin.

"Where's Temel?" I asked, changing the subject.

"He won't be joining us for dinner," Dorothy said. "He has another assignment to fulfill." She removed several Styrofoam tubs and aluminum platters with plastic lids from the bags. Steam wafted from the various containers, and I closed my eyes to breathe in the satisfying aroma. Maybe my hunger drove me to relish every bite, but I had to believe the Jordanian meal ranked as one of my all-time favorites. My friends seemed to agree with me. Lisa moaned with satisfaction after each bite, and Trendon, though hesitant at first, soon devoured several plates' worth of food.

"What is this?" I asked, pointing to the container holding a green salad with kalamata olives, cucumbers, eggplant, and cubes of white cheese.

"It's called Halloumi Salad," Abelish said, the corners of his mouth rising slightly with a smile. "It comes from *kharoof.* I mean from goat."

Trendon's smile dimmed. "What was that?"

Abelish's eyes widened. "Baaaaah."

"Goat? Like goat cheese?"

"Mmmm." Abelish rubbed his belly. "Very good goat, yes?"

Trendon timidly pushed the cheese around the container with his fork.

"And that," Abelish nodded to an almost empty container of rice and meat. "Mansaf," he said proudly.

"Mansaf," I repeated, licking my lips and offering him a meager smile.

"Enjoy it," Dorothy said. "You usually don't get Mansaf unless you're celebrating a holiday or a wedding."

"Elma, my niece, is best at Mansaf." Abelish kissed his fingers to make his point.

I ate until my stomach ached from all the food and then sat back and watched Trendon eat way too much. When he finally offered a disgusting belch to announce the end of his meal, most of the aluminum and Styrofoam containers were all but licked clean.

Dorothy patted Abelish on the shoulder. "Well done, old friend."

"Of course." He bowed and then carried his own empty plate out of the room.

"Amber, don't," Dorothy said to me as I began to clear the table of garbage. "We'll clean this up in a little bit."

I hadn't been given much time to think since arriving in Jordan, but now, with my stomach full, my thoughts became clear. "What do all those pins on the map represent?" I asked.

Dorothy fished a stray olive from the remaining salad platter and nibbled on the end. "Locations of artifacts and other relics around the globe." She stood and motioned for us to join her by the map. "A purple pin indicates the location of a relatively dangerous artifact and one still under our guard."

"Why purple?" Trendon asked.

"I like purple," she answered flatly. "Yellow pins are just guesses. Either we have a hunch or some of our research has led us to believe in the existence of artifacts in the general area. Whatever the case, we really don't know if anything at all exists there, but we keep a pin to mark it nonetheless."

"And the red pins?" I already knew what the answer would be.

"Lost artifacts," she answered. "Either they've been taken from their location by known enemies, or they've somehow mysteriously vanished without our knowing."

There weren't as many red pins as yellow or purple, but there were still quite a few. My eyes drifted toward the Philippines, where, among several purple pins dotting the small island nation, I noticed the blaring red one poking out from the area near Mt. Arayat. An enormous feeling of guilt welled in my chest. Maybe we did the right thing by locating the Tebah Stick, but part of me wondered if that pin would have remained purple had Trendon and I not involved ourselves with the search.

"And you guys really think there are that many artifacts in the world?" Trendon asked.

"Hard for you to believe?" Dorothy asked with a smile.

Trendon leaned his shoulder against the map. "You know what I mean? I believe there are historical . . . things everywhere. Every culture has them. That's what museums are for. But come on, most of the time they're like broken pieces of pottery or clay weapons."

"What's your point?" I asked, inwardly wanting Trendon to stop leaning on the map. He was bound to uproot a few pins.

"He doesn't have a point," Lisa muttered.

"Yeah I do." Trendon's voice rose with agitation. "My point is all of these pins don't just represent clay pots." He waved a hand across the map. "They're supposed to represent things similar to the Tebah Stick. Artifacts with magical powers . . ." His voice trailed off, and he wiggled his fingers mockingly. After all we'd witnessed, Trendon still struggled with letting go of his suspicions.

"I see," Dorothy said. "And that seems far-fetched to you."

"I agree with him," Lisa said softly.

No surprise there. Lisa didn't want to believe any of this, and if anyone had the right to question it, it was she. She'd never seen the Tebah Stick at work.

"How about you, Amber?" Dorothy nodded toward me.

"I think I believe it. The world is full of so many mysterious things. People have buried them or hidden them in safe locations. Why would they go to all that trouble?"

"Can I make a comment?" Trendon politely raised his hand.

"Of course you can," Dorothy said. "Everyone's opinion matters. Even the ones that conflict with others."

"Other than the Tebah Stick, which—sorry, Amber—I never really saw perform all those magic spells . . ."

"They weren't magic spells!" I snapped.

"Whatever. Other than that incident, how do we know any of these artifacts can do anything amazing? How do we know they're not just junk or sentimental things weirdos thought they should bury? Has anyone tested one out?"

"You mean used the artifacts' powers?" Dorothy asked.

"Yeah. Like grabbed the Tebah Stick and hopped aboard a condor or something crazy. I mean, there's no proof any of that stuff works. All we're doing is following you around like baby ducks."

Normally, Trendon's harsh words would've irritated me, but I found myself agreeing with him. We were just following her around. What if there wasn't a point to it?

Dorothy didn't respond. Instead she glanced at the map, deep in thought.

"So what artifact are you keeping here?" Lisa asked.

I followed her gaze to where a purple pushpin poked up from Amman, Jordan.

Dorothy's lips parted, and she nibbled nervously on the corner of her lips. "I was wondering when you'd notice that. Nice observation, Lisa."

"Right here. Right beneath us." Trendon jabbed at the floor with his thumb.

She nodded, and my eyes widened. I looked at Trendon, and though he wore a ridiculous grin, I could tell he had begun processing this new bit of information. Even Lisa appeared curious.

Dorothy sighed. "All right, Trendon, you've won your chance for proof."

"I don't follow," Trendon said. "What are you talking about?"

Dorothy winked. "You'll see."

13

A variety of paintings of biblical scenes clung to the walls on either side of the hallways as the four of us took a long walk to the opposite end of the compound. One of the paintings depicted the familiar battleground with David squaring off with the giant Goliath. The Philistine army flanked Goliath in evident celebration, while David stood alone, his fingers closed around the leather straps of his sling. Farther down hung an image drawn in charcoal on some sort of papyrus and protected in a small glass frame. In it, a soldier rode in the back of a chariot with a sword extended in his hand. The horses pulling the chariot stood with their hooves held high in the process of trampling down upon a woman.

"Yikes. That's a nice drawing," Trendon said.

"I was about to say the same thing," Lisa added.

"That image is over two thousand years old. That's Jezebel, the evil queen who put a bounty out on Elijah's head. And the champion in the chariot is Jehu. This drawing is of the fulfillment of Elijah's prophecy." Dorothy pointed to where several dogs stood in the background of the painting. "Jezebel spent most of her life persecuting the prophets, and Elijah said that she would one day be torn apart by dogs."

"Lovely," Trendon said out of the corner of his mouth. "Elijah certainly was a peach, wasn't he?"

Dorothy only smiled.

At the end of the hallway, two soldiers with machine guns flanked a door with a secured digital keypad lock and a camera protruding from the wall. Dorothy entered the code, and the door gave off a pneumatic hiss as it opened.

Concrete flooring echoed beneath our feet as we entered the room, and fluorescent lights buzzed overhead. Two large, metal platforms stood near the rear of the room, with opaque glass cases centered upon them. Metal conduit snaked out from the platforms to where a laptop computer and various microscopes and cleaning utensils rested on a desktop. Numbers and symbols crawled across the screen of the laptop.

"So what is all this stuff?" Trendon grabbed the mouse and moved the cursor across the screen.

"Careful, Trendon!" Dorothy snapped, flashing a rare sign of annoyed emotion. Up to that point, she had acted relatively passive, but upon seeing Trendon barge up to the desk like an ornery rhinoceros, she instinctively lost her cool.

"You can't be serious," I said, tugging on the back of Trendon's shirt and causing him to stand straight. "You barely walked into a room, and you've already started touching things."

Trendon released his grip on the mouse and backed away cautiously. "I wasn't going to click anything. I thought those numbers were some sort of idiotic screen saver."

"It's not a screen saver, and please don't touch anything unless I tell you to." Dorothy knelt in front of the computer and right-clicked the mouse. A small menu screen popped up, and the series of numbers and symbols vanished, replaced by a graph with hundreds of peaks and valleys.

Dorothy positioned the laptop where all three of us could see the screen. "What you're seeing here is a graphing of electromagnetic energy. This graph represents ninety-six hours of uninterrupted data collection."

"On what?" Trendon blurted.

"On that." Dorothy pointed toward the steel platforms. "Go on." She urged us forward with a flick of her chin. "You can take a look. Just don't touch anything."

I walked forward, a little unsure of what to expect, but eager nonetheless. Trendon and Lisa followed as we approached one of the platforms. Steel hinges clamped the glass case to the top, and a tiny bulb of green light flashed from a black console on one corner. Distinct electrical sounds, high-pitched and continuous, hummed from beneath the case. A long wooden post at least two inches thick, splintered and broken at one end, lay beneath the glass.

"Any guesses on what that is?" Dorothy asked, still hovering over the computer with her eyes glued to the monitor.

"Uh . . . a microphone." Trendon smudged his index finger across the glass.

"Guess again."

"That really wasn't my guess," he mumbled.

My eyes narrowed. I examined the object, taking in the details and allowing my brain to focus. "It's some sort of spear."

"Well done," Dorothy said.

"Why is it dangerous?" Lisa asked. I fell silent, trying to remember any significant stories where a spear had been the primary mention.

"The wielder of that spear killed over eight hundred men all by himself," Dorothy answered.

"Eight hundred?" I asked. "That's impressive." Dark and somewhat evil, but impressive.

"This was Adino the Eznite's weapon. We found it in a tomb in Israel a few years ago."

"So what?" Trendon said. "Why does that make it an artifact? Couldn't the guy who killed all those men just have been really good? Plus, it doesn't make the spear an artifact, it just means the dude was awesome."

"Not when he only swung it once." Abelish entered the room quietly and stood halfway between the door and us. "Dorothy, do you think it wise to let them be here?"

Dorothy looked up from the monitor and stared at the glass case. She entered a series of keystrokes on the computer, and the green bulb on the platform switched to red. The humming electrical buzz immediately ceased, and the glass case opened. "They need to see some viable proof." She crossed the room to where we stood. Placing her hands on her hips, she stared at Abelish defiantly. "This is proof."

"But they're just kids," Abelish said.

"I don't mean to interrupt you guys, but I'm cool with coming back later. How about the rest of you?" Trendon glanced at Lisa and me. His suggestion actually surprised me at first. Trendon never worried about interrupting people. "We don't want to cause any trouble." I then realized what really drove his intentions. Trendon fixed his eyes on Abelish's completely covered wrists.

"Nonsense. You're not causing trouble. Abelish is just being overprotective, which is exactly how I want him to act. However, you've been thrust into this conflict and have had your lives and your families' lives threatened. I have complete trust in you and therefore feel it is perfectly fine to give you an example."

Trendon pulled out his phone and focused the camera in on the opened case.

"No pictures!" Abelish grabbed for the phone, but Trendon, either too swift or too protective of his prized possession, quickly moved it out of reach.

"Take it easy. I'm not gonna upload it on Facebook or anything." I watched as Trendon wiped his phone with his shirt. If I could've punched him without causing a scene, I would've done it right then.

"It's okay, Abelish. Trendon, put away your phone, please," Dorothy said. Trendon grinned innocently, finished his discreet cleaning of his phone, and then stuck it back in his pocket. "Now, go ahead and pick it up."

The smile quickly vanished when he realized what Dorothy had asked him to do. "Me? Why me?"

"I want you to see for yourself. It's not going to hurt you."

"What's it going to do? Make me turn colors or something? Break out in a . . . rash?"

I gritted my teeth and glanced at Abelish. Apparently he hadn't picked up on Trendon's more-than-just-subtle hinting.

"You should be fine," Dorothy said. "Come on, now. It's time you realized what's out there."

"Really?" I asked. "You're gonna let him hold it." It felt like a bold move on her part. What would the spear really do to him?

"I don't need to hold anything." Trendon slowly backed away from the case. "I know perfectly well what's out there without sticking my hand in there."

"I thought you didn't believe in mystical artifacts," I said, but my heart had begun to thud sharply in my chest. I glanced down and realized I'd been absentmindedly wringing the end of my shirt in my hands.

"Why don't you pick it up?" Trendon pointed at me.

"I think you should be the one to hold it first," Dorothy said soothingly. "You need proof to disperse your doubts. And I promise you, this will do it."

"I don't want to . . ."

"Just pick it up!" Lisa said, growing impatient.

Trendon shot out a hand and closed it around the wooden shaft of the spear. Lifting it, he tested its weight, shook it like a bottle, and then twirled it over and over in his hand. "It's lighter than I thought it would . . ." He stopped and cocked an eyebrow, staring suspiciously at the spear. Gripping the wood with two hands, he raised it up to eye level. "Can you guys feel that?"

I couldn't feel anything, just a pit in my stomach. Trendon's face made me nervous. I'd seen too many movies where someone picked up something they shouldn't and then exploded. I didn't want to think about it, and I focused in on the realization Dorothy would never try to hurt Trendon.

"It's a . . . h-h-hot," he stammered. "I mean, not really hot like a . . . no, wait." He breathed rapidly. "More like really cold. It feels so cold and . . . and . . . heavy!" His voice rose with excitement.

"Heavy? But you said it was light." Lisa reached out and steadied Trendon, who had begun to wobble slightly. "Maybe you should put it down."

"I'm not talking about heavy as in weight. It feels . . . um . . . what's the word? Thick, or maybe . . ."

Dorothy gently pried the spear from Trendon's fingers, and he immediately breathed a loud sigh of relief.

"Whoa!" he exclaimed. "That thing is . . . whoa!"

"Do you see now?" Abelish asked, sounding agitated. "Can we stop this charade?"

"That was unreal!" Trendon sniffed and wiped his nose. "I felt I could slice through the wall with that thing. I could've, couldn't I? If I swung it, I could take the whole place down."

I felt myself smiling at how ridiculous he sounded. "Don't be stupid, Trendon. You wouldn't even know how to swing that thing."

"Says you! Here, give me that back, and I'll show you." Trendon reached for the spear, but Dorothy withdrew it.

"Amber's right, I'm afraid," Dorothy said. "The weapon is incomplete, and though you can feel its power, you can't control it."

"Baloney! Give me that thing!" Trendon lunged for the spear, and Dorothy, out of surprise, relinquished her hold without a struggle.

"Boy!" Abelish growled, shoving Lisa out of his way to get at Trendon. "If you damage that . . ." Trendon backed away, holding the spear out defensively.

"What are you doing?" I shouted.

"Settle down, folks. I'm just gonna show you something," Trendon said. Abelish held his ground but didn't advance aggressively as Trendon's eyes flashed from him to the desk.

"You've lost your mind," Lisa said. "Please give that back before he kills you!"

Trendon's eyes caught sight of something interesting, and he bounded toward the desk chair, toting the spear in his hands.

Abelish moved forward, but Dorothy held her arm in front of him, preventing his advance. "Abelish, let him," she muttered.

Trendon pulled the chair out from the desk and centered it in front of us. "Now, watch me pound this thing to dust." His lower lip curled down with sheer determination as he held the spear high over his head and swung it down with all of his strength.

The spear bounced off the chair, which sent it

shooting across the floor toward the desk. Trendon lost his balance and toppled face-first onto the floor.

I couldn't stop myself from laughing. The look on Trendon's face had been so priceless. He rolled over, rubbing his nose viciously and blinking back tears of pain.

"Why didn't that work?" he groaned.

Abelish lifted him off the floor and pulled the spear from his fingers. "The weapon is incomplete. To harness its power, you would need to reconnect the spearhead."

"Well, where is it?"

The warrior flashed a quick glance toward the other platform. A stone spearhead, approximately the size of my hand, rested beneath the glass case. Upon seeing it, Trendon rushed over to the platform and tried to remove the covering.

"I haven't released the lock on it for good reason." Dorothy held up her hands to steady Abelish. "Easy, he's just curious."

Abelish looked ready for blood. "He's treading dangerous waters. No more of this!"

"Chill out, dude!" Trendon said. "I know what I'm doing. Let's reconnect the spearhead on that puppy and set me loose on Baeloc!" Lisa and I joined him at his side, staring down upon the piece of stone.

"Why not?" Lisa asked. "If it's so powerful, why haven't you used it?"

Dorothy smiled and put her arms around our shoulders. "Now you see the dilemma that faces us every day. A weapon like this could be used to prevent wars. Keep the peace. But what if it doesn't work the same anymore?

What if thousands of years lying dormant have caused it to become volatile? Unpredictable? The wielder of such would be taking an enormous risk."

"The Tebah Stick hadn't been used since Noah, and it worked fine. I think." Trendon looked at me for approval, but I didn't know whether or not the Tebah Stick had worked properly.

"Maybe," Dorothy agreed. "But there have been other cases where an artifact backfired and people were killed because of it. Issues always arise when dealing with the items we have to deal with."

"I can't see any issue that would keep you from trying," Trendon said.

"Okay. For starters, where did that power come from?" Dorothy asked.

"From . . ." Trendon hesitated. "What do you mean? You don't know?"

She shook her head. "We can speculate. There are passages in the Bible telling of Adino's great deed when he killed eight hundred with this spear, but then the question still exists: How did the power come to be inside the spear?"

"Well, it's probably from . . ." I began to say, but Dorothy kept me from completing the sentence.

"Is it?" A smile faintly lingered on her lips. "Are you so sure? Maybe it is from a higher, heavenly source, but without complete knowledge, there's a risk involved. Weapons created by evil means can only yield evil results. One thing is for sure, a weapon like this that can be wielded by either good or evil is no longer fit for this world."

"That really happened?" Lisa asked. "Someone killed eight hundred people with one swing?"

"Yes, and it didn't just happen once. Several people used this spear in battle and saw miraculous results. At one time, it was believed to be the greatest weapon on the earth. These artifacts are why that map with all the pushpins upstairs exists. This is why we risk our lives and unfortunately your lives as well." She frowned with regret. "Imagine Baeloc in possession of a complete weapon such as this. Imagine the anarchy that he could cause."

"But that's what he's trying to do right now," I said. From what Dorothy told me about the Book of Despar, Baeloc had every intention of wreaking havoc through-out the world as payback for his misery. "Baeloc is searching for weapons like this."

"Worse," Abelish said. "Far worse. Much more pow-erful weapons capable of terrible deeds. This is why we must stop them."

"And why we must keep you hidden, Amber," Dorothy whispered. "Now can you see why we did what we did?"

"So is that why you're testing it?" Lisa asked. "To find out if it's good or bad?"

Dorothy's smile widened as she returned the spear to its platform. After entering a code on the computer at the desk, the glass case closed and the green light on the monitor flashed on.

"We're gathering a little information, but again, it's incomplete. This weapon can never be officially tested," she said.

"What's it doing here then?" I asked.

"We're waiting for the right time to destroy it," she answered.

"Destroy it?" Trendon blurted. "You would do that?"

"Of course," Abelish said.

"What a waste." Trendon stared longingly at the spear. "You'd think you could at least try to swing it. Break some junk or something."

"You need a Destroyer," I whispered. "Someone in the society capable of destroying an artifact. Is that what you're waiting for?" I remembered my discussion with both Dorothy and Cabarles months ago about the different levels of membership within the Seraphic Scroll. Dorothy was a Collector, someone assigned to locate and move dangerous artifacts. Cabarles had been one of the Sentries who protected the locations of secured artifacts. The last assignment was that of a Destroyer, a person capable of removing dangerous artifacts from the earth.

Dorothy patted my arm. "Nothing gets past that brain of yours, does it? You're absolutely right. A Destroyer must be the one to remove an artifact such as this from existence. But we're not waiting for him." She glanced at Abelish. "He's already here."

Abelish shifted his weight and looked away. "Dorothy," he whispered, almost ashamed. "I . . ."

"You're a Destroyer?" I looked at Abelish now with more intrigue. Because of his robe and turban, I couldn't see behind his ears where I now believed he possessed the tattoo of a scroll rolled back with ancient Egyptian markings. The mark of a Destroyer.

"Can we at least watch you destroy it?" Trendon asked, not sharing the same reverence. "Maybe you could swing it at a wall or something, just for fun."

"He's not ready." Dorothy's smile weakened. "He needs more time."

"More time for what?" Trendon asked.

Abelish's head jerked toward him. "The artifact must be destroyed, but there's a danger with releasing its power. A danger I agreed to face when the time is right, but I'm not ready just yet."

Trendon leaned next to me and under his breath whispered, "I bet it's because of his rash."

"Trendon!" I shouted. "I can't believe you said that!"

Abelish's expression faltered, and Dorothy sighed. He looked at her briefly and then, after a moment's hesitation, removed his turban and completely revealed his face. Lesions pocked his chin and neck. His skin looked distinctly altered because of some disease. Abelish also removed his gloves and pulled back his sleeves, revealing even more of the unsightly skin abrasions. They were everywhere and looked extremely painful.

"I am a leper," Abelish said. He watched Trendon, but not in a challenging way. It looked as though he feared what Trendon might say about this new revelation.

Trendon didn't immediately respond but looked away from Abelish's skin. I did as well, hoping my action came across as respect for him. "A leper?" Trendon questioned. "Like with leprosy?"

"Generally, that's what constitutes a leper," Dorothy said.

"Is it contagious?" Trendon probed further. I glared at my friend but could tell he was trying his best to sound respectful.

Abelish re-covered his arms and face. "You have no need to worry about my disease. It will not harm you. Now, I think I should be going." None of us spoke as Abelish bowed respectfully to Dorothy and left the room.

I knew a little about leprosy from a discussion in class a year or so ago. The disease actually affected millions worldwide, including many in the United States, but it was treatable. Most people could receive medications to lessen the effects. By the looks of Abelish's skin, he had never received any such treatment.

"I didn't mean to be rude," Trendon said.

"Oh, of course not!" Lisa scolded.

"Hey, I just . . . whatever." Trendon turned to Dorothy. "How did he catch . . . ?" He wiggled his fingers by his neck.

"Easy, Trendon," Dorothy soothed. "I always forget about your quirks. Abelish has had this condition since he was very young."

"I feel terrible." I stared at the ground. "I hope he didn't think we were judging him because of it."

"He's learned to live with his disease, and he's okay, but it is also what defines him," she explained.

"Isn't there something he can do? Like treatments?" Lisa asked.

"He underwent the necessary medication and was almost able to rid his body completely of the disease. But then he stopped the treatments a few years ago."

"Were they too expensive?" I asked.

Dorothy shook her head. "Not for Abelish."

"Then why stop?" Trendon leaned across the glass case, staring at the spear.

"He no longer saw the need. Abelish took on the responsibility of a Destroyer in our society, and unfortunately, that is almost always a death sentence."

"What?" Trendon asked, looking up from the case. "Why does he have to die?"

"Destroying an artifact is not a simple task. It can't just be broken into pieces. It must be burned, but when that happens, certain artifacts have been known to release deadly energy. Destroyers understand this risk and devote their whole lives to this cause. They prepare themselves physically, mentally, and spiritually, for they don't know what will happen to them once they carry out the task. Since our society began, many people have been called upon to assist with the deadly but necessary assignment of destroying dangerous artifacts."

"Do they have to have a disease to be a Destroyer?" Trendon asked.

I rolled my eyes, but Dorothy answered before I could scold him for his bluntness.

"That's an interesting question. No, having a disease is not a requirement, but every Destroyer in our history has been a leper. Abelish volunteered for this assignment. He has prepared himself to do what is needed and no longer cares about his external appearance or even the discomfort his leprosy causes. It's all part of the transition to becoming a true Destroyer. Even I don't understand the internal changes he has made to truly embrace his calling. But I do know he is almost ready. Initially, he had planned to carry out the work of the Destroyer on Adino's spear, but now it would appear his services are needed for another artifact."

"The Tebah Stick," I whispered.

"Perhaps."

"It seems so harsh," Lisa said. "What about his family? Doesn't he want to live for them?"

"Other than his niece, he has no family. At least none that he keeps in touch with. Abelish is one of my dearest friends. We've been through a lot together, but when we deal in a world where cruel people desire to use weapons for evil, there are sacrifices to be made. He is one of the bravest people I have ever known."

An uncomfortable silence settled in the room. My thoughts circled about the mysterious Abelish, and I felt deeply sorry for him. His willingness to endure unspeakable hardships from his disease and even face death to stop evil men like Baeloc instantly earned him my respect.

"That's just idiotic!" Trendon finally ended the silence in true fashion. "He doesn't need to die. Just give me a few minutes with that spear and I'll change this whole mess around. Believe me, I'd know exactly what to do. There's no need to—"

I clamped my hand over Trendon's mouth, fed up with his constant jabbering. "You're done, buddy. Okay. I think all that power went right to your head."

"Yeah, and there's nothing else in there to kick it out," Lisa said, joining me.

"Disgusting! Did you just lick my hand?" I yanked my hand from his mouth and wiped the saliva on my jeans. Trendon smiled with feigned innocence.

"All right, you three. You've had a long and exhausting day. I'll take you to your rooms, and you can get some sleep." Dorothy stepped between us just as it was about to turn ugly. "Tomorrow's a big day," she said. "You'll finally be able to talk with your parents."

14

"What are you, a grizzly bear?" Trendon asked when I finally opened the door and stared groggily out into the hallway. "We've already eaten breakfast."

I could barely remember a few details of my dream. I remembered the creatures and the cave and something else . . . a light of some sort . . . but everything else seemed fuzzy. I had been too exhausted when my head hit the pillow, and I didn't wake up until I heard Trendon pounding on my door at 11:00 a.m.

"I was so tired," I groaned, rubbing the sleep from my eyes.

"And of course you have a bigger room than any of us." Trendon pushed his way through, Lisa following behind him. "And you have carpet!" He stomped as he circled, taking in the details. "I swear my room's slanted. Everything rolls to one side. And you probably have clean sheets too." He checked beneath the comforter and chuckled. "You're such a princess."

"Shut up." I punched him in the shoulder. "It's just a place to sleep."

He plopped on the bed and lay back on my pillows. "Come on, get ready. Dorothy's going to keep her promise."

I brushed the tangled mess of hair from my eyes and blinked at him in confusion. What was he talking about? Trendon seemed too interested in fluffing my pillow to offer me an answer, so I glanced at Lisa for an explanation instead.

"Our parents," she whispered.

A knot formed in my stomach. I should've been excited to talk with them, but I didn't know what to say to them. Would they be angry? I had practically lied to them for months, and that wouldn't sit well with them, especially my dad.

Trendon and Lisa waited outside while I showered and found a few changes of clothes in my closet and my backpack resting on the floor. The drawer by my bathroom sink contained a toothbrush, toothpaste, and everything else I needed to feel clean and normal. I mentally made a note to thank Dorothy for being such a gracious host. Yes, she had brought us here against our will, but at least she had remembered to give us deodorant.

Our rooms were right next to each other on the third floor of the hotel. We took the elevator down and met Dorothy on the main level. She then led us to a conference room down the hallway behind what used to be the check-in lobby. Abelish sat in the corner of the room pressing several buttons on a piece of electronic equipment when we entered.

"Because of security dangers, you'll be given ten

minutes to speak to them. I wish I could give you more, but for now, it will have to do." She seemed all business. Just by her stern expression, I could tell she didn't want any of us to call. "You are not to speak of Baeloc or make mention of any of our names. Be brief and discreet. They'll want to know how things are going, and I strongly suggest you tell them you're doing just fine."

"Why?" Trendon asked. "You want us to lie? We're not doing fine. This is the worst vacation ever."

"Vacation!" Abelish's eyes lit up as he looked away from the equipment. "That's good. Tell them that."

"But we're not on a vacation," Lisa said in a calm voice. "They already know that, don't they?"

Dorothy's lips drew tight. "If I feel at any moment you might accidentally reveal information to them, I will immediately disconnect. Furthermore, and this is critical,"—She took a deep breath—"you are not to tell them your location. Nothing about the flight or anything about the country. Are we clear?"

I nodded vigorously. Trendon gave an unenthusiastic thumbs up, but Lisa only shook her head and looked away.

"Don't hang up on my parents," she whispered.

"If you follow instructions, Lisa, I won't have to. Now, Amber, you're going first. You guys, why don't you step outside and give her some privacy."

For some reason, I expected Dorothy and Abelish to leave along with them, but they didn't. Abelish dialed some numbers into the phone and handed me the receiver while they listened in with a pair of headsets.

The first couple of rings droned in my ears like a hollow-sounding gong. My eyes itched, and I could tell my hands were shaking noticeably. By the third ring I had managed to regain control over myself, then my mom picked up and I about lost it.

"M-mom?" I asked, my voice cracking.

"Amber, thank goodness! Its about time," she answered. "Dale, pick up the other line. It's your daughter." After a few seconds of silence, I heard the phone click, and my dad joined.

"Amber, is that you?" he asked.

"Hi, Dad. How are you?" There was something about hearing their voices. I was a mess inside and had been since my conversation with Joseph in my dorm room, but I had managed to put up a wall of fake courage. My parents had a way of crumbling that wall in an instant.

"Busy," my dad said. "Which is good. I'd rather be busy than the alternative."

I smiled, grateful for such a brave father. Through all of this craziness he could play it off as normal. I knew he was doing that for my benefit. "Busy, huh?" I asked, wiping a few tears from my eyes.

"Yeah, well, as long as there's money to be made, I'll have plenty to do."

"Dale, stop talking about work and let her speak," my mom said. "They told us you'd only be able to call for a few minutes, so we'll let you do all the talking. How are you doing? How's the trip?"

I swallowed. Trip? Had Dorothy coached my parents as well on what they should ask? "Um . . ." Unsure of how to respond, I looked at Dorothy. She raised her eyebrows expectantly. "Good, I guess. Kind of crazy." Why hadn't Dorothy given me more instruction on the proper code? I didn't want to break her rules, and I certainly didn't want to reveal our position to Baeloc by slipping out information.

"Crazy?" my mom asked. "Are you getting enough sleep?"

Why didn't my mom sound more troubled? I had expected her to be borderline hysterical. "Yes," I whimpered. "Are you?" Enough of this talk about me. I needed to know how they were being treated by Dorothy's people.

"Oh, you know how much your father snores," my mom said, and then she giggled.

I stiffened and ground my teeth until my jaw squeaked from the pressure. I felt a hollowness form in my stomach. Something wasn't right.

"I don't snore, Amber," my dad fired back. "How's the food there? Is it greasy?"

"It's okay." My heart began to pound. I looked at Abelish listening intently in his headset, and my eyes slowly fell upon Dorothy. Her whole demeanor had changed. I could see tears in her eyes, and she looked genuinely sad. At that moment I knew the truth.

"All joking aside, Amber. You need to call us more. Emails don't cut it," my mom said. "I know you're busy getting your education, but we need to be kept in the loop of all your activities. It's one thing to be enrolled in that school away from home, but I don't care for all these extracurricular events."

I covered my hand over the receiver and glared at Dorothy. "They don't know?" I whispered.

Dorothy closed her eyes. "Amber, tell them good-bye."

"Make sure you stay in the group," my mom continued. "And don't eat anything unless you know it's been cooked thoroughly." I could hear my parents bickering back and forth on the other end on what they should be talking to me about, but I was no longer in the conversation. I felt betrayed, and my eyes welled up with tears.

"Mom, Dad, I have to go."

"Already?" my mom asked.

"I love you guys."

After a few complaints from my mom, my dad cut her off and answered, "We love you too. Call us in a week."

The line went dead.

I waited a full minute before exploding. "You lied to all of us!"

Dorothy stood. "Amber, we had no choice. You would've come, I think, but there was no way we could get Trendon and Lisa unless we told them about their parents."

"I can't believe this." Dorothy had managed to stoop even lower. I had finally come to grips with the fact she had lied to my parents for their protection, but that wasn't even true. "Where do they think I've gone?"

"La Trobe University," Dorothy answered.

"Australia?" I asked.

"Yes. They own a fairly well-known study-abroad

program for up and coming archaeologists."

"I know about La Trobe!" I snapped. It was my dream university. The school I hoped to one day graduate from in archaeology. For the past three years I had read pamphlets and articles online about the school, and now supposedly I was already there. Along with a hollow feeling of betrayal, I also felt dejected. Why couldn't we have gone to La Trobe for real? That would've been a much better trip.

"We gained clearance from the school, and administration handled all of the details," Dorothy continued.

"And the emails my mom talked about receiving? Did you write those as well?"

That question appeared to darken Dorothy's mood even more as she nodded. "Listen, we didn't lie about everything. I said we were protecting your parents, and that is the truth. There's still a risk Baeloc will strike out at them, and your parents are being watched by some of our best men. We needed to ensure their safety, and we're doing that. They just don't know about the circumstances."

"I should've listened to Joseph!" I said.

Dorothy appeared to finally understand. "Ah, I see. And what did Joseph tell you? Is this why you've been looking at me differently?" she asked.

"He just said I shouldn't trust you."

"But that's not all. What else did he tell you, Amber? Go on. Let's hear it."

Not yet. I didn't want to tell her what he told me just yet. I needed more time to think it through, and I didn't want to say anything I would regret even though I was so angry. I stood from the table but rested my hand on the phone. "I want to call them back."

She didn't respond but only stared at me and rubbed her fingertips on her lips.

"No," Abelish said after the silence seemed too much for him. "I can't let you do that."

"Yes you can. I want to tell them more."

Clearly amused by the absurdity of my suggestion, he removed his headset. "What will you tell them? Where we've taken you? What good would that do?"

"I don't want to lie to my parents!" I shouted.

Dorothy stared at Abelish for a moment. "Get them back on the phone," she instructed.

"You're making a joke?" he asked.

"No. Amber's in charge here. If she wants to call her parents and tell them about her situation, I'm not going to stop her."

"Really?" I asked. Was she bluffing?

"Sure, kiddo, but you need to know the consequences that could happen with revealing anything about our situation."

"I understand," I said flatly.

"Do you? What do you think your dad will do once he knows the truth? Who would he involve? If I know anything about your father, it's this: he will stop at nothing to help his daughter. He will risk his life for her, and make no mistake, Amber, your mother's and father's lives are in danger. But if you want to call them and bring them up to speed on everything, I won't stop you.

If that will help mend our relationship, I'd be willing to sacrifice our security. I don't want you to hate me."

I squeezed the receiver and ran my fingers over the buttons. I didn't hate her. She had ticked me off and I had lost some trust in her, but I couldn't hate Dorothy. I thought about her father, who had disappeared into the Amazon when she was a toddler. I didn't know most of the details of that story, but I understood he had taken a risk going off a lead on an artifact. Dorothy had gone her whole life without her father. Could I live knowing my impetuousness cost my dad his life?

"Okay," I said. "I won't tell them anything, but I want to at least talk with them longer and say good-bye in my own way." What if I never saw them again? Did I really want my last conversation with my parents to have ended so abruptly?

Dorothy agreed, and although Abelish grumbled yet again from her leniency, he dialed the number. Though surprised to hear my voice so soon, my parents were very happy for a few extra moments. I spoke to them about school and Trendon. They liked Trendon. They had never met him in person, but his behavior always made them laugh. My parents were healthy and from their knowledge doing just fine. I cried the entire conversation but managed to keep that from them. When the phone call finally ended after fifteen minutes, I felt better. I didn't forgive Dorothy and didn't think I would for a while, but part of me understood why she did what she did.

Wanting to give us time to cope with the news, Dorothy left us alone for the rest of the day. We had our freedom to walk about the compound as long as we stayed within the gates, and in the evening, she dropped off our dinner in my bedroom. Three bowls of steaming soup with cold chicken sandwiches and a plate of cherries, figs, and apples made up the meal. Everything tasted delicious.

All things considered, Trendon and Lisa handled the news of their parents better than I had.

"It really didn't surprise me that much," Trendon said as he slurped through his soup.

"That they lied to us about our parents?" I asked in disbelief.

He shrugged. "My parents are too busy to care one way or the other."

"But you freaked out back at the museum!"

"Yeah, so?" Trendon wiped his chin. "Just because my parents don't care doesn't mean I want to spend my weeks in this dump. I have better things to do with my time."

I stirred my soup and fished a potato from the steaming yellow broth. "How about you?" I asked Lisa.

She had been mostly quiet listening to our conversation. "I think I knew Dorothy was lying from the beginning. I just couldn't buy it."

"Really?" I asked.

"You don't know my dad." She nibbled on her roll. "There's no way anyone could stop him if he knew I were in trouble."

I had wondered why Lisa had handled the news so calmly. She had been quiet and frustrated but never acted truly worried about her parents.

"Why didn't you say something?"

"I don't know. I was scared, I guess."

"Does this mean you really hate me now?"

"I don't hate you." She looked shocked.

"You said yourself back at the museum you thought I was keeping things from you. And now you're caught in the middle of it all." I glanced up from my plate. I hadn't eaten much, but my anger had settled somewhat having spoken with my friends. If they could come to grips with what Dorothy had done, then certainly I could.

"I know now it's not your fault. And seeing Joseph and hearing Dorothy and him talk about how much danger you were in made me realize this wasn't some dumb activity from class. I know I said some things that hurt your feelings, and I'm sorry for that. I also couldn't live with myself if something bad happened to you guys. If Dorothy thought keeping us together would help you out, then I suppose the least I can do is just be there for you. Even if it means lying to my parents."

I dropped my spoon and reached over to hug her around the neck. It was one of the best feelings I had felt in a while, and we squeezed each other and cried while Trendon watched us with a bewildered look on his face.

"I'm so glad you're here," I whispered. "You too, Trendon." I shot out my arm and dragged him into a group hug. Though at first he tried to resist, he soon gave in, and the three of us hugged each other and laughed. For the moment, I did indeed feel safe.

15

The time crawled by agonizingly slow. None of us had ever been to Jordan, which should have been exciting, but we were never given the chance to explore the country. Confined to the security of the compound, most of the areas outdoors were off limits. We had plenty of food supplied by Abelish's niece along with an assortment of exotic fruits and vegetables. Dorothy provided us with changes of clothing, semi-hot showers, a few board games, and a television in each of our bedrooms. We saw Abelish from time to time walking the hallways, but Temel had been absent from all of our meals. I hadn't seen him since first arriving in Amman, and I began to wonder what had become of the peculiar man.

I had yet to do much research. Not that I had a lot to go off of, but I still felt at a loss for concentration. Unlike the Tebah Stick in the beginning, I already knew what the Architects were looking for. Joseph had already told me. The Fire of Elijah was some sort of weapon used by the prophet and passed on to his successor. Baeloc knew of its location but couldn't get to it without the aid of the Tebah Stick. My role was simple in the whole ordeal and had already been laid out. Perhaps it was the lack of mystery behind the artifact that caused me to neglect searching for more, but honestly, most of my thoughts that week had been on my own family. I constantly worried about them, and it brought on exhaustion. At night, I would plop on my bed and almost instantly fall to sleep worrying about my parents.

Yet my nightmares had grown in strength. No longer did I wake in the mornings confused by the clouded memory of them; all of the details vividly manifested themselves throughout the day. Each of my nightmares contained certain elements without fail.

The first was the new cave. I had finally determined the location had nothing to do with Mt. Arayat anymore. They were far too different. The walls in this cave were made of a different type of stone, and the ceiling seemed almost too heavy. It didn't make sense to me no matter how many times I pondered the dream throughout the day, but I felt more claustrophobic in the cave from my dreams, as if there was no sunlight above the stone ceiling.

The second element was the creatures. There were always two of them. One in front leading me to my destination and one behind, lurking in the shadows. I could never see the one behind me, but its existence was one of the truths of my dream. It was there, and it was close.

The third was the Tebah Stick. The artifact had become one of my permanent appendages once I fell asleep. It was the one piece of the dream I always felt relieved to see. Yes, I knew by holding it I had somehow taken it from Baeloc's possession, but I also felt relief knowing the artifact kept the creatures at bay.

The last element disturbed me the most. Abelish had joined my nightmares immediately after my learning of his disease. The warrior would appear beside me from time to time but would never acknowledge me outright. I would watch him walking with slow strides, no longer cloaked or hooded, with the full evidence of his leprosy in plain sight. He wore a solemn expression, one of resolution as if he were headed to fulfill his destiny.

No matter how many times the dream recurred, I never reached my destination. I would always come close, just a few steps from grasping it, but I could never make out what it was. I supposed stress had caused the nightmares, but I began to wonder about their true meaning. Because of fear, I never told anyone about them.

When a week had passed with no indicators of a break from the cramped hallways of the compound, Trendon finally pitched a fit.

"That's it!" he shouted after I beat him and Lisa in a game of Hearts. "I've had it with this dump. I don't care what's outside. It could be a freaking nuclear explosion. I'm going for a walk, and I'm finding me a McDonald's."

"They're not going to let us out of here," I said, shuffling the cards. "Not until it's safe."

"Safe?" Trendon smacked the mattress. "This place is a hole! Do you know how many cockroaches live in my room? Eight. I've named them."

"Why don't you just squash them?" Lisa asked, reaching for the cards and beginning her deal.

"Yeah right, and then what would I do? They carry so many diseases!" He stood and walked to the window, which overlooked a courtyard three levels below.

"Trendon, we all want to go home, but Dorothy knows best," I said.

"No she doesn't," Trendon said. "We're like prisoners."

"We're not prisoners. We got to call our parents, didn't we?"

Trendon made a raspberry sound with his lips and folded his arms. "People in prison are given a phone call too."

"Are you going to play or what?" Lisa asked, staring down at Trendon's cards.

"No, I'm done. I can't keep losing at card games." He left the window and hopped back on the bed. "I can't believe I'm going to say this, but I think I want to find out some answers about the Fire of Elijah."

Hearing Trendon voluntarily admit his interest in archaeological research was like hearing someone reveal a deep, dark secret. He was brilliant, and I always believed if he would just apply himself to archaeology with the same amount of focus he gave to hacking computers and playing with his phone, he could easily become a great archaeologist. But that just wasn't his nature.

I looked at Lisa, wondering if she would object, but she appeared eager as well. "Okay," I agreed. "We'll need some research material. Like a Bible, an atlas, maybe some encyclopedias."

Dorothy had an extensive collection of books in one of the conference rooms on the main level. We looked for her and Abelish for over an hour, but apparently they had both left the compound. Figuring she shouldn't mind us trying to help, we took the liberty of accessing her library without permission.

For two hours we sat at a table poring through books, reading various articles on Syrian culture, cemeteries, and lore, while filling up pages of notes. It felt like a final exam, and I loved every minute. Even Lisa participated by plotting out possible grave sites on a large topographical map of Syria.

"I don't know what you guys know about Elijah, but that dude was hard-core," Trendon said, glancing up from his reading. He had spent most of the past hour leafing through a small, pocket-size copy of the Bible.

"How do you mean?" Lisa crowded next to him and looked over his shoulder at the pages.

"He didn't mess around. Worship an idol? He burned you with fire. Ask him too many questions? He burned you with fire. Look at him cross-eyed—"

"He burned you with fire?" Lisa asked.

"You're so brilliant." Trendon snapped his fingers. "The Bible is full of him bringing fire down from the sky and gobbling people up. Chip?" He offered the bag of chips to Lisa, who politely declined.

"Elisha did some pretty amazing things too," I added. "He once parted the waters of a river and walked on dry land." I had focused most of my research time reading the two leather books I had brought with me in my backpack. They seemed to contain verses identical to those in Trendon's Bible, but I felt compelled to search for differences. I had managed to read through both books of Kings for a second time, but other than the small circles on the random verses, I found no variations.

"Like Moses?" Trendon asked.

"Exactly. And after he had been dead and buried for over a year, some Israelites dropped another dead man down in Elisha's grave, and when the body touched Elisha's bones, the dead man stood up and walked away, completely healed."

Reverent silence settled in the room. Trendon looked at me and then at Lisa before asking, "Do you really believe all that happened?"

I didn't know how to answer that. It seemed beyond fantasy. They were mysterious men who performed seemingly impossible wonders. I did know one thing was certain: if they could indeed call fire down from heaven, then the artifact we were looking for was more dangerous than any other weapon.

"I keep thinking about Abelish." Lisa stood and searched the wall for another book. At the mention of Abelish's name, I noticed Trendon nervously glance away from his reading. "He's basically giving up on life. Don't you think that's terrible?"

"Definitely. It is terrible." I nodded in agreement.

"I don't know," Trendon mumbled. "It's not too shocking, if you ask me."

I watched Trendon for a second, looking for any signs of sarcasm, before I erupted on him. "He's going to die! Are you so insensitive to see that? He's sacrificing his life to destroy an artifact. It's sad!"

Trendon scooted a foot or so away from the table and held up his hands defensively. "Whoa, easy! It is sad. I'll give you that. And just because I don't want to stand around the guy that much, doesn't mean I'm insensitive."

"That's exactly what it means!" Lisa said.

"Look, he's had leprosy his whole life. He's had to cover his body and hide his disease from the world. He's got no family other than some niece. What's he got to live for? I still think dying to destroy an artifact is stupid, and I don't necessarily want to see him do it, but I can kinda see his point."

Lisa and I didn't press this issue because I realized I agreed with him. I had never learned Abelish's age, but I estimated he had probably entered his mid to late forties. His whole life had been one filled with suffering. He was ashamed of his appearance, and I could only imagine the pain the leprosy caused. Dorothy had told us, Abelish wasn't yet ready to follow through with his assignment, but he was close. Maybe he believed he would find peace in death, but I couldn't help but feel sick about it. It seemed to be a miserable end to his life.

We silently returned our concentration to our research. After another thirty minutes of page turning, I could take it no longer. "I know what you're going to say, but I want you both to look once more at these verses." I passed the leather books across the table to Trendon and Lisa. I hated to admit defeat, but I had failed to find any variations in the text. Four circled numbers of verses inconsequential to anything related to Elijah's Fire.

"Not that garbage again," Trendon groaned. "We've already read them plenty of times."

I ignored him and urged Lisa to read them aloud.

1 Kings 3:5—In Gibeon the Lord appeared to Solomon in a dream by night: and God said, Ask what I shall give thee.

1 Kings 3:8—And thy servant is in the midst of thy people which thou hast chosen, a great people, that cannot be numbered nor counted for multitude.

2 Kings 3:6—And king Jehoram went out of Samaria the same time, and numbered all Israel.

2 Kings 4:5—So she went from him, and shut the door upon her and upon her sons, who brought the vessels to her; and she poured out.

I wrote some of the words on a piece of paper and studied them. Not one of them spoke about Elijah, and only the last verse dealt with Elisha. But that story happened far before his death. Why were these verses important? Had someone marked them by mistake? I jotted down the numbers of the verses, thinking that could lead me to an answer.

3:5, 8; 3:6; 4:5

I felt stupid. The numbers were worthless. Trendon thought I was wasting his time returning my focus over and over to the circled passages, but I couldn't help it. Dorothy wasn't the one who sent them to me, so the books had come from another source.

"Joseph," I whispered. "I think he sent these to me."

Trendon shifted in his seat. "Why would he send you those books? He's a moron."

"He's not a moron. He knows a ton about what's going on. He probably wanted to play it safe, so he stuck the books in my mailbox so that I would research them later."

"Oh please." Trendon crumpled his bag of chips. "You don't know if he sent you those, and even if he did, you're acting like he's some mystical psychic who just happened to know you'd use the books to solve the puzzle. We're talking about Joseph here, the captain of the foosball gang! That guy's worthless."

"You don't know anything!" The blood had raced to my neck, and I could feel my cheeks flushing with color. "Maybe the verses aren't the clue, but that doesn't mean Joseph isn't trying to tell us something here. What we need to do now is figure it out."

"Stop fighting, you two," Lisa said. "It doesn't matter who sent the books. What matters is that we have them."

But it did matter. Maybe not to them, but this matter was monumental to me. Joseph was reaching out to me in his own way. I couldn't ignore it.

For the rest of the evening, Trendon and I hardly spoke. No longer interested in plotting burial sites on a map, I filled my time diligently searching the leather books. Trendon had given up on reading the Bible, and on the whole search, for that matter. The annoying whistles and sounds of him playing a game on his iPhone consistently broke our concentration.

With Lisa's help, we used several tactics we had learned in Dorothy's class to search for hidden watermarks within the books. We carefully lit matches beneath the pages hoping the smoke would reveal wax rings. We couldn't find lemons in the hotel but discovered a few strange citrus fruits called etrogs in a basket near one of the conference rooms. Using some of the juice from an etrog, we brushed the pages, searching for any differences or raised edges to appear. Though I felt proud of our efforts, we didn't find any clues.

When I finally surrendered my search, it was after 9:00 p.m. The compound had fallen quiet, and we had yet to see any signs of Dorothy or Abelish checking in on us. I looked at Trendon, who hadn't spoken to me in over an hour.

"I'm going to bed," I said, gathering up my belongings and heading toward the door.

"Good," Trendon mumbled.

I rolled my eyes but didn't argue. I didn't want to fight with him anymore. It was exhausting, and no matter how clear I explained things, Trendon was too stubborn to listen. Why did he hate Joseph so much? Why couldn't Trendon just let things go? Yes, Joseph had lied to us and nearly got us killed, but he had changed. We were in this together and needed to help each other. When going up against an enemy as evil and dangerous as Baeloc, one couldn't have enough friends. I didn't really expect them to be best buddies, but I just wanted Trendon to try to forgive him. I couldn't be the only one.

16

Though the weather in Jordan was pleasant and cool and Abelish had told us to expect chilly nights, my room felt quite stuffy. There was no air conditioning, and just one small, oscillating fan covered in dust stirred the air around my bed. I had felt this sort of discomfort before while sleeping in Cabarles's spare bedroom in the Philippines. My mouth had dried out, and I'd needed a drink of something cold, and preferably not the water from the sink. Dorothy had warned us not to drink it unless we boiled it. The real reason I hadn't slept lay about my bed. I had tried once again to search for hidden messages in the books but had failed. Maybe it was time to ask a professional. I knew Dorothy had a far better knowledge on encrypted messages than I could ever dream to own, and I decided to seek her out despite the late hour. There was a chance she had not returned from wherever she had gone with Abelish, but I didn't care about the risk.

"Lisa," I spoke to her door, trying to keep my voice

low yet loud enough she would hear. "I'm going looking for a vending machine and to talk to Dorothy. Do you want to come?"

She opened the door after a few minutes and appeared to consider the invite. Even after little sleep and dressed in pajamas, Lisa somehow managed to look immaculate. She had painted her fingernails and styled her beautiful red hair in a plaited braid. I had no idea our bathrooms even had fingernail polish. Glancing at my own cuticles, I shuddered. Neglect. No other word better described it.

"No, I think I'll pass. I'm pretty tired," she said.

"I could bring you back something if you want."

She thought about the gesture and then shrugged. "If you find an orange soda, I'd be ecstatic."

"Deal."

Though Trendon and I had ended the night on a negative note, I still wouldn't have minded his companionship. But after knocking six times on his door and being unable to wake him, I decided I would go alone.

The halls were empty and quite creepy as I tiptoed toward the stairwell. On the level just below our rooms, I passed a couple of soldiers heading toward the opposite end of the compound. They paid no attention to me as they hurried through the doorway by the empty swimming pool. More soldiers joined them. Where were they going in such a hurry? I wondered if I should follow them. Instead, I quietly walked in the direction from where the two soldiers had come. I found an ice machine and what looked like a snack machine in one of the rooms, though I didn't recognize any of the snacks. As I fumbled in my pocket for change, I heard a voice rising from down a side hallway. I froze and listened. Creeping forward until I could see the light seeping out the bottom of a room, I strained to pry into the conversation.

"Where are you keeping them? Why haven't you let them go?" Dorothy's voice rose with anger. "We made a deal, and you got what you bargained for!"

No one responded to her intense questioning, which made me wonder if the conversation was taking place on a telephone. If so, who was she talking with and why was she so angry? Pressing my ear against the door, I honed in on her voice, blocking out all other sounds around me. It was probably wrong of me to spy on her like this, but something told me to continue listening.

A long pause in the conversation followed, and I could hear some sort of scratching sound. What was going on? Dorothy then laughed, and she was joined by Abelish.

"We don't have our men," Abelish growled.

More silence. I strained my ears to listen, but no one seemed to be talking and then . . .

"Out of the question!" Dorothy said. "You think we would bargain for her? You're out of your mind. This will not end well for you. Any of you. She'll never be part of the equation. You'll never find her." Her voice trailed off, and I held my breath. Find who? Who was she talking about?

The door suddenly opened, and I fell sideways into the room on top of Dorothy. The two of us stared at each other for what felt like several awkward minutes. Behind her, tied up in a chair, was a pale-skinned Architect. His arms and legs were bound tightly, but his hands had some mobility, clinging to a pencil and paper. Various messages littered the floor at his feet. Standing next to the Architect, holding what must have been a phone to the man's ear, was Abelish. In Abelish's other hand, he held a gun, the deadly barrel pointed at the man's chest.

The Architect's eyes widened with surprise when he saw me. He then jabbered some hideous words into the receiver before Abelish had time to cut the power to the radio. Abelish swore as he tossed the device away and backhanded the Architect across the mouth. Dorothy forced me out into the hallway.

"Wait here!" she ordered as she slammed the door. I stood there, frozen to the floor, my feet unable to move from the spot. What was going on in there? Why did Dorothy and Abelish have some creepy member of the Qedet tied up? I swallowed as I pieced together another question. Who had been on the phone?

The door once again opened, and a calm Abelish, with his gun returned to the holster at his side, beckoned me through the doorway with his gloved index finger. He held the phone in his other hand with a piece of strange equipment attached to the receiver. For just a moment, I recalled the memory of my nightmare and the role Abelish played. I imagined his damaged skin covering his chest and wondered how close he was to fulfilling his destiny.

"Come in." Abelish spoke sternly, but I didn't feel threatened by his voice. The Architect had gone, the scribbled messages removed from the floor, and the chair rested neatly next to the wall with a few other wooden pieces of furniture. Any evidence of the strange encounter I had witnessed earlier had been wiped clean.

"Amber, what were you doing out there?" Dorothy stood at the far end of the room next to another closed door. Even in the darkness, I could see the distinct shape of a gun jutting out from her hip. The room was nothing more than a gutted hotel suite with a few wooden chairs, a bathroom, a closet, and some electronic equipment in the corner. The door she stood by must have led to an adjoining bedroom. She looked on the verge of exploding with anger.

"I . . . uh . . . was buying something to eat from the vending machine when I heard you talking." I looked around the room. Was the Architect still tied behind the closed door?

"He's in here." Dorothy nodded to the door. "Stop worrying about him." She knew my thoughts. The images of the man tied up with a gun pressed to his body still burned in my mind. It certainly felt like some sort of torture scene from a terrible movie. Was that what Abelish and Dorothy had been doing to him? Torturing him for information? "You listened into our conversation?" Her arms folded tightly at her waist.

"I didn't mean to at first," I whispered. "I was just wondering why you were so angry." I watched Abelish cautiously. What if I hadn't shown up when I did? Was he about to use his gun to kill the Architect?

"This is why we should always operate in the more

secured parts of the compound. Careless," Abelish said, examining a few of the connectors on the phone. "We never used to be this careless."

"Be quiet, Abelish," Dorothy snapped. "Amber, were you spying on us?"

"It was an accident. But why was that man tied up in here? What were you doing to him?"

"That's none of your business!" Her hands dropped to her side, clenching in evident frustration.

"None of my business?" I fired back. "I thought this whole situation was my business. Did he break in? Was he trying to get to me?" I immediately tried to erase the face of that Architect from my mind. I thought about him slinking in the shadows, chattering in his hideous language, searching for me. Had more of the Architects found a way into the compound?

"No," Dorothy answered. Her hands stopped clenching, and she somewhat relaxed. "It's not like that at all. He's our prisoner, and we brought him here for questioning."

I breathed a sigh of relief but then stiffened. "But you weren't questioning *him*." I remembered the phone held to the prisoner's ear. "He was just writing the answers. Who was on the phone with you?"

Dorothy's expression faltered, and she temporarily looked horrified by my question. "You need to leave now."

"You said, 'you'll never find her.' Who were you talking about?" I couldn't leave the room now. Not without answers, when I knew her conversation pertained to me in some way.

Dorothy glanced at Abelish, who merely shrugged in response. "It was nothing. Don't worry about it." She crossed the room and placed her hands on my shoulders. I could feel them trembling.

"Then why did you need Abelish?"

"I needed him to ensure the call went untraced," she whispered.

"Who were you talking to?" I demanded again.

"No one of importance. No one you need to trouble yourself over."

"It was Baeloc!" Trendon's voice erupted, seemingly coming from nowhere. Abelish spun around and pulled out his gun once again. Dorothy reached for her weapon as well as I twirled around, looking for Trendon.

"Trendon?" I asked. "Is that you?"

The closet door in Dorothy's room opened, and Trendon stumbled out, trailing snack crumbs in his wake. "I heard the whole thing," he said, chomping on some unknown pastry. "From start to finish."

"Both of you should be ashamed of yourselves! You've been in here the whole time? What if something had . . ." Dorothy stopped and covered her mouth.

Abelish once again returned the gun to his side but appeared to keep his hand at the ready. "Who are these kids?"

"Sorry, Ms. H., but you've got some explaining to do." Trendon stood beside me as we stared down our teacher together. "Ask her what really happened to the Tebah Stick."

Dorothy's eyes closed tightly. "Please . . . I . . ."

"What did you do?" I asked. How could this be happening? Joseph had been right all along about Dorothy. First she lied about our parents, and now this.

"Yes, that was Baeloc on the phone, and what you heard sounded treacherous, but it's not exactly as you think." She shifted sideways and then plopped down in one of the chairs. "We were trying to trace the call to make a connection."

"Enough," Abelish growled. "Stop involving them!"

"Whoa, Abe, if you haven't already noticed it, we have a way of involving ourselves. Just make it easy on yourself." Trendon elbowed me playfully.

How could Trendon think this was humorous in any way? Dorothy a traitor? I felt hollow and lost. Who would protect us now that we couldn't trust her?

"The gig is up, Ms. H. Time to spill the beans. You've been a naughty girl." He grinned, apparently proud of his discovery.

"Trendon!" I hissed but then rubbed my eyes in frustration.

"What?" he fired back. "I've been here the whole time. Abe and Dorothy called Baeloc on that phone, and they used the other dude in the chair as a translator. They asked questions, and he answered them from Baeloc. They were talking about how Dorothy had given Jasher the Tebah Stick while they were in Spain together. Now, apparently Baeloc is trying to negotiate for you. But don't worry, Dorothy's not giving in . . . yet."

"Are you finished?" Dorothy asked, her voice more under control than before. "May I speak now?" Trendon waved a hand permissively. "I see you're already coping with the idea I've joined the dark side, but before you get too excited, let me explain. Just after the incident in the Philippines, Jasher and Baeloc captured six members of the society. And with the Tebah Stick in our possession, it gave us a hefty bargaining chip. It took us a couple of months to arrange a meeting for the exchange. The men for the artifact."

"Are you crazy?" I asked but then caught myself from speaking more of what was on my mind. I still had some respect for my teacher, even if it had started to dwindle. Abelish had an ugly scowl on his face, clearly disgusted by the liberties Dorothy took to fill us in. I didn't care if it made him upset. We had every right to know.

"We never intended to go through with it," Dorothy continued. "The purpose of the meeting was to establish contact and give Temel an opportunity to track them. We weren't even supposed to have the artifact anywhere near the location, but our plan backfired. One of the most trusted members of the society betrayed us by delivering the Tebah Stick to Baeloc."

"Whoa. Big shocker there," Trendon said under his breath.

"Yes," Dorothy said with irritation. "You're right. Lately double-crossing has become the theme of our organization, but I assure you I am not one of them. Neither is Abelish or Temel. We're on your side. We were trying to save lives, but then it went terribly wrong. We didn't waste time though, holding to the hope that our assumptions about the artifact were accurate and that they wouldn't be able to use it without you. That's why we came after you as quickly as possible, and we got to you just in time."

"Is Emmanuel the person that double-crossed you?" I remembered the name Abelish had mention on the airplane just after he had killed the pilots.

Dorothy nodded. "Indeed he *was*." She emphasized the last word, and I gathered what that meant.

"Emmanuel's dead, isn't he?" Trendon asked.

"Yes," Dorothy answered, nodding at Abelish.

"You're a stone-cold killer." Trendon's eyes narrowed as he stared at Abelish. "Is that what all you Destroyers do?"

Abelish's scowl darkened. "Nice to have me on your side, don't you think?"

"For now," Trendon mumbled. "I know this will sound harsh, even coming from me, but how could you risk losing the Tebah Stick to save a couple of soldiers?"

"These were not just random men; these were some of my dearest friends." Dorothy gazed up at Trendon.

"Oh, sorry. Then it makes it all worth it." Trendon took a cautious step away from Abelish, undoubtedly still wary of his leprosy, not to mention the gun at his side.

"You don't understand!" Dorothy's voice rose. "Cabarles was one of them."

I caught my breath. "Cabarles? Not him! You never said that. What are they doing to him?" In a short period of time, Cabarles Godoy, Dorothy's contact in the Philippines and the one-time sentry of the Tebah Stick, had become my trusted friend. Trendon and I would've been lost without him. I looked at Trendon and could see the news equally troubled him.

"We don't know. But Jasher has been known to employ different tactics when it comes to questioning. It wouldn't surprise me if he's resulted to torture."

"But Jasher's dead, right?" Trendon chimed in.

"That's right." Dorothy pressed her eyes together. "I still keep forgetting that."

"No matter," Abelish said. "Baeloc will be much worse than Jasher."

I sat down next to Dorothy. "You did what you had to do. It makes sense."

"Does it?" Dorothy asked. "Am I justified for risking the lives of millions, maybe even billions of people for a few friends? Lately I've been questioning my decisions."

Losing the Tebah Stick into the hands of a madman was not her best move, but what would I have done had I known I had a chance to save Cabarles? Would I have risked it? I thought about my closest friends and my family. If it were Trendon in Baeloc's clutches, suffering all sorts of torture, would I have hesitated to help?

"You did the right thing," Trendon whispered, beating me to the answer. "Don't blame yourself."

"So what do we do now?" I asked. "Did we mess everything up by showing up at the wrong time?"

"No, it's not your fault. We didn't have a really good plan of attack anyway. But speaking of which," Dorothy said, facing Trendon, "how did you get into my closet without me or Abelish knowing?"

Trendon shifted awkwardly. "Uh . . . I've been in there for almost two hours."

"No." Abelish shook his head. "That's impossible. I would've known. You're too noisy."

"Yeah, well, you didn't know. I was up looking for something to eat when I saw Dorothy heading for this room. I thought it would be really funny to sneak up on her and scare her, so I waited until she went into the bathroom and then I picked the lock." He held up his school ID card, now completely bent in two. "It wasn't that hard. These doors are old. I was thinking of jumping out and scaring you, and then I heard Abelish come in. I realized he was probably packing a gun or his sword and would most likely shoot me."

Dorothy's mouth fell open slightly. "Yes, you're lucky you didn't jump out because he *would've* shot you."

"Without a second's hesitation," Abelish added.

"How did you call Baeloc, anyway? How do you have his number?" I asked anxiously.

"We don't have his number, but Cabarles has a two-way communication device. It's like a cell phone, but it can only receive and transmit calls from this phone." Dorothy held up the cumbersome piece of electronics and pointed to a black, circular device connected to the mouthpiece. "The scrambler makes it untraceable. It's what Temel used back before we took you to the airport. We've made contact before but had no means of communicating with Baeloc. Then we caught a break with *him*." Dorothy nodded toward the closed door, behind which the pale-skinned Architect must have sat tied to a chair. "Temel found him earlier this evening near the airport in Ben Gurion."

"But how do you know for sure who you spoke with was Baeloc? They all sound like a bunch of crickets. What if that dude was lying?" Trendon asked.

"It's possible, but it doesn't really matter. There's no way to get our men out. Baeloc won't accept any form of trade, unless, of course, we offered you." Abelish winked at me. "And though I've been tempted because of your constant meddling, Dorothy here outright refuses."

"So what's going to happen to that guy?" Trendon nodded at the door.

"Why do you care?" Abelish asked.

"I guess I don't, but . . ."

"Yes he does!" I quickly chimed in. "We both care. You're not going to kill him, are you?" No more deaths. I didn't want to be a part of such a grisly operation. Did they not value human life? I felt terrible for Abelish's calling, but that didn't mean I approved of how easily he killed his enemies without a second's hesitation.

Abelish regarded the door for a moment. "The thought had crossed my mind."

"He's not going to kill him." Dorothy reached over and reassuringly patted my hand. "Despite what you may think of us, we're not out to kill everyone who opposes our cause."

"But this doesn't mean we're letting him go," Abelish said. "We're not ignorant."

"Yes, we have to be careful. I don't know what exactly he said in the phone when he saw you, but he probably alerted Baeloc you were with us. That will change how things play out from here on."

"Is that why all of the soldiers were running to the opposite end of the compound?" I remembered how they had hurried away, not paying me any attention.

"Beefing up security," Abelish said. "Our special guest required it."

"Do you have any idea of where Baeloc is camped?"

Dorothy sighed. "Not really. And we can't take a risk of exposing ourselves to the Architects. If they know where we're hiding, they'll come for you, and their numbers far exceed ours."

"What about him? Couldn't he have some answers?" I stared at the door and felt the gaze of everyone else in the room following my lead.

"The Architect?" Abelish asked. "He would never tell us what Baeloc knows. The Architects are too obedient to his commands."

"Yes, but so was Sherez, wasn't he?" I asked. "And now he's on our side."

"Our side," Abelish scoffed. "Or he's just laying an intricate trap to catch you."

Trendon stood next to me. "We could ask him a few questions. Maybe he'll slip up and leak out some information."

"While writing?" Abelish chuckled.

"Come on, dude, give us something!" Trendon growled. "We're trying to help, and right now you guys stink at this stuff. Let us take a shot. Or are you forgetting who actually found the Tebah Stick in the first place? If you ask me, you should've never taken us off the job of protecting it."

Abelish slowly folded his arms at his chest. "What's that supposed to mean?"

"Oh, nothing," Trendon said with an innocent smirk. "Just pointing out the fact that we'd probably not be in this mess if Amber and I were in charge."

"Watch it, buddy," I whispered under my breath.

One of Abelish's eyes began to twitch beneath the tightly wrapped fabric of his facial covering.

"Settle down," Dorothy said. "I don't know if letting you two talk to him is such a good idea. He's dangerous."

"Dangerous?" Trendon flinched. "It's not like he can do anymore damage. You tied him up good, didn't you?"

"I tied him myself." Abelish's eyes narrowed, challenging Trendon to question further.

"It's my life that's at risk here, right? Then I should have a say in how things go. And I say we deserve a chance to ask him some questions." I looked from Abelish to Dorothy but kept my jaw clamped tight.

Dorothy tapped her finger on her lip. She had already broken all the rules by putting us this deep in the situation. "Okay. I'll give you five minutes." She stood and stared defiantly at Abelish as if challenging him to refuse. Abelish, however, only nodded and joined her by the door. "Keep your distance though," she said, resting her fingers on the doorknob. "And when we say the time's up, you can't argue."

But before Dorothy had pulled the door wide, I could tell from her eyes something was terribly wrong. Her hand slipped from the knob, and she swore under her breath. I had barely glanced through the opening when Abelish pulled out his gun and charged past us.

"Get back!" he shouted.

The Architect's chair sat overturned in the center of the room. His bindings lay strewn across the floor, and the sound of flapping curtains drew our attention to the window, where someone had dangled the bedsheets out the opening. Somehow the Architect had managed to cut himself free and had escaped.

Dorothy's prisoner was gone.

"Tied him up yourself?" Trendon asked. It was bad timing on his part, but Abelish never replied. Dorothy shoved Trendon and me onto the bed.

"Stay here!" she ordered, and then both she and Abelish were gone, leaving us all alone in the hotel room.

"What a mess." Trendon sighed. "They sure run a tight ship, don't they?"

I kept silent as I stood and stared out the window. It wasn't a far drop, two stories at the most. The window overlooked an inner courtyard of the hotel compound. Hedges and dried-out shrubbery in desperate need of watering decorated the lawn, and some beach chairs circled a small, murky swimming pool with a diving board. The only way out of the courtyard was through a rod-iron gate by the far wall at least fifty yards from our window. A few armed soldiers stood by the gate, and I could see the faint glow of cigarettes held in their fingertips. Anyone could've made the jump from the window and easily survived, but where would he have gone? Through another window on a lower floor? Surely the man would've caught the attention of the soldiers standing guard and they would've stopped him. Unless . . .

With the question still lingering in my mind, I turned to ask Trendon what he thought and nearly fainted.

The Architect stood in the room with a knife held to Trendon's throat and his hand clamped tightly over his mouth.

17

No sounds or else.

The words had been hastily scribbled on a torn piece of paper before the Architect tossed it on the bed.

I stared at the knife practically digging into Trendon's chin and noticed the Architect's shaky hand. Was he nervous or excited? Like Sherez and Baeloc, it seemed impossible for me to read his expression. The Architects always seemed to grin, but from the way this man's eyes shot back and forth from the doorway to me, he knew he didn't have much time. Abelish would return at any minute, and the encounter would end violently. Trendon's eyes seemed wild and alert as though he were on the verge of doing something similar to what he had done at Papa B's restaurant. Capturing his attention, I shook my head slowly and mouthed the words "don't do it." Fortunately, Trendon understood and obeyed.

I wondered if we could hold out long enough for Abelish, but then I began to imagine how things would play out. Would the Architect value his own life and go quietly, or would he be willing to sacrifice it for Baeloc's cause? I then remembered the broken conversation I overheard between Dorothy and Temel. She had instructed Temel to protect me at all costs. Had Abelish received similar instruction? If Abelish returned, he would attack the Architect to protect me, which would make Trendon vulnerable.

"Okay," I whispered. "What do you want us to do?"

The Architect's eyes flashed with anger and he gripped the knife tighter.

"Sorry!" I held up my hands submissively with the hopes of easing the tension. "I won't say anything else."

Couldn't he see the impossibility of this? We were deep within the compound, with Dorothy's soldiers searching for him. There was no easy way out of the hotel. Maybe he already understood, but it didn't stop him from shoving me out into the hallway first with Trendon following closely behind.

"What are we going to do?" Trendon whispered. "This dude's—" His voice muffled and fell silent as the Architect clamped his hand over Trendon's mouth.

Three elevators stood a few yards down the left hallway. Above each of the elevators were unlit triangle lights pointing in opposite directions. The Architect smacked the call button on the wall, and we waited several angst-filled moments until the center door opened and the three of us stepped in.

"Don't go up," I whispered. "They'll catch you for sure." We were at least two levels above the main lobby with the most obvious exits. Above us were four floors of hotel rooms and soldiers patrolling the hallways. It was a deathtrap. Maybe not for me, but most certainly for Trendon.

Trendon's eyes widened with shock. "I'm sorry, am I missing something here? Are we all working together now?"

The Architect choked out a few disgusting words and pressed the button marked "L" for lobby.

When the door opened, we found the lobby level empty, and I caught the faintest hint of a smile on the Architect's lips, the first obvious emotion I could see out of any of them. With his foot, the Architect probed me out through the entryway.

A large mirror with an ornate frame hung on the wall at the end of the hallway. Its mirrored glass reflected our looks of exhaustion and uncertainty. The Architect, however, wore a triumphant expression. But as we approached the mirror, someone else appeared behind us in the hallway.

Temel.

It was the first time I had seen him in over a week. At the moment, I was the only one who noticed him creeping around the corner, resembling some sort of stalking animal from the Discovery Channel. As Temel reached behind him to pull out his gun, the Architect noticed him in the mirror. Whirling around, the Architect ducked behind Trendon just as Temel fired.

"No!" I screamed. A brilliant flash of light lit up the end of the muzzle, and the bullet whizzed just inches above Trendon's head before shattering the mirror behind him. Temel dropped the gun in shock, but the bullet never touched Trendon.

Now with a renewed sense of urgency, the Architect dragged Trendon out of the hallway as Temel charged toward us.

"He almost shot me!" Trendon shouted. "That moron!"

"Please!" I begged once we made it out into the parking lot. "Just let him go. You want me, not him." The unwanted image of Trendon being shot replayed itself over and over in my mind.

"Whatever, Amber, I'm not going anywhere. Stop trying to talk to this freak," Trendon said.

Using the two of us as a barricade, the Architect directed us away from the compound and onto a main road. Vehicles of all sizes zoomed down the street, blaring their horns, swerving to avoid us. None of them stopped though. Maybe they were driving too fast to notice the knife held at Trendon's throat. We walked for several blocks and passed buildings locked up for the evening. I kept expecting Temel to appear racing toward us, but he never showed. Judging by the way he had crept along the hallways of the hotel, I imagined him looking for the right moment to strike, intent on not making the same mistake twice.

Eventually a blue-gray taxi with a bright glowing sign on the hood came to a stop next to us. The passenger side window lowered, and a man peered out, speaking something foreign. Before the driver could realize what was going on, the Architect yanked the door open and forced us into the front seat next to him.

"No. Nope. Sorry. No." The driver rambled on and on, staring at the Architect's knife. "No English. No drive. Out! Out!"

Hissing, the Architect held out the knife, and the taxi driver didn't wait around long enough to see what would happen next. Screaming in his foreign tongue, he fled out of the door and crossed the road, just barely dodging several speeding vehicles.

"What now?" Trendon asked. "You wanna drive and let Amber hold me in a headlock?" The three of us sat wedged between the emergency brake and the slightly ajar car door.

The Architect pulled the door closed, making it even more uncomfortable. After several seconds of eyes darting around the tight quarters of the taxi, he pointed at me and jabbed his chin toward the steering wheel.

"Me?" I asked in shock. "I don't know how to drive!" I hadn't even been enrolled in drivers ed for a month! I had driven with my dad a few times, but never unsupervised and certainly not in such a highly trafficked area. Plus, the taxi's steering wheel was on the wrong side of the car!

"I can," Trendon said. "But I'll have to sit in your lap so you can keep choking me." He chuckled at his own joke.

More hideous words vomited from the Architect's mouth as he shook his head in answer to Trendon's suggestion.

Trendon held up his hands apologetically. "You

could hold Amber and let me try to maneuver this thing. Or," Trendon continued, "we could all just wait here for trigger-happy Temel to shoot us with his amazing aim."

At the mention of Temel's name, the Architect released his hold on Trendon and clamped his hand over my mouth; placing the knife's edge under my chin, Trendon climbed over the emergency brake and squirmed around for a moment to get comfortable in the driver seat.

"Okie dokie. Piece of cake." On accident, he flipped on the windshield wipers.

"You really can drive this thing?"

Turning off the wipers, Trendon triggered the turn signal and then drummed his fingers on the steering wheel impatiently. None of the other drivers seemed interested in slowing down long enough to let him pull out. The Architect anxiously swiveled his head from the front to the rear of the taxi and shouted more words at Trendon.

"Blabbity blah!" Trendon fired back. "You sound like a badger."

A few blocks behind us, Temel appeared on the sidewalk, looking in the windows of the various buildings along the road. Where was Dorothy? Maybe Temel had taken off after us without alerting them. If that were the case, he was our only hope of being saved. Once again I realized he had been charged to save only me. I'm sure he cared about Trendon somewhat, but if it came down to keeping me out of Baeloc's clutches or letting the Architect take the two of us without a fight,

Temel would most certainly attack. I knew, trapped in such a cramped space as the front seat of the taxi, one of us would be killed. And one in three odds weren't great.

"Drive!" I shouted.

Trendon jumped. "Easy! No one's slowing down enough to let me out."

"Hurry up, Trendon!"

"Why are you in such a rush? Or did you forget where we were going?" Trendon pressed on the gas. "There, finally!" The taxi lurched forward, right in front of a speeding truck, which barely swerved to miss us. The truck's driver laid on his horn as the taxi accelerated. I turned and watched as Temel shrunk on the sidewalk, and, within moments, he was gone.

18

The drive took close to five hours, and the taxi's tank had just enough gas to enter Hama, Syria, after filling up only once at a service station. We had passed through Damascus three hours earlier. Joseph and Dorothy had severely erred on the burial site of Elisha. If they were to start looking now, which I assumed they would once they discovered Trendon and I had been taken, they would be over a hundred sixty miles south from us. My hopes of them somehow finding and saving us from the Architects faded away into nothing. The Orontes River glimmered like a black snake beside the road as we passed through the bustling city of Hama. Stone-arched entryways appeared around every corner, and beautiful pomegranate trees sprang up along the riverbed.

The memories of Kendell Jasher's mansion in Istanbul were still vivid in my mind when Trendon pulled the taxi up to Baeloc's domain. Jasher's home had been a palace with spacious rooms, illustrious marble columns, and massive stone fountains. Of course, Temel and his

gang demolished the mansion in a few short hours, turning it into nothing much more than a smoldering crater.
Looking upon the fortress of Baeloc, I couldn't help but
wish for the crater. Like Jasher, Baeloc lived within a
gated community, but by the looks of things; no one
else inhabited the other homes along the road. Potholes
marred the ground as the taxi crawled to a stop in front of
a several-storied, brown brick house. Snarling gargoyles
perched upon the upper levels overlooked the grounds,
and creeper vines zigzagged across the sidewalls and
dangled over the balcony. The building looked more
like an abandoned manor on a plantation. There were a
few trees on the lawn, but they were withered and old,
with twisted, ash-colored branches. All of the windows
across the façade of the house had been filled with more
of the brown bricks and mortar. There seemed to be
nothing hospitable about Baeloc's home.

The entryway door opened, and several Architects
flooded out, carrying weapons. Our captor stepped out,
leaving us temporarily alone in the taxi, and the silence
broke with the sounds of excited cackling.

Covering my ears, I stared at Trendon. "You've got
to make a run for it! They only want me. They'll kill
you."

"I'm not leaving you, so shut up!" Trendon reached
over and opened the glove compartment. He pulled
out a tire gauge and held it out like a knife. "Think I
could poke their eyes out with this?" He jabbed it at the
window.

I smiled faintly. "Please listen to me." The sound

of the Architects' twisted voices grew in volume, and I glanced over my shoulder as Baeloc appeared in the entryway. His arms stretched out and embraced the Architect responsible for delivering us to him. "There are too many of them, and you won't be able to make a difference now. Maybe you could make it back down the road and signal for help."

Trendon looked out the back window of the taxi. It was at least a half mile down to the gate, and I couldn't remember seeing too many vehicles along the road outside of the neighborhood. Could he really outrun all of the Architects?

Turning back to face me, he shrugged. "Nah. Why would I volunteer to run?"

We stared at each other for a moment, and then I fell into his arms and squeezed him with all of my strength. I could feel his body shaking from fear, like I was sure he could feel mine. We had been in dangerous situations together before, but even when we faced the creatures in Mt. Arayat, I had never felt as defeated as I did outside of Baeloc's home. Why had I been so stupid? All the time I was trying to protect Trendon from an attack back at Dorothy's compound, I could've been yelling for help. I had let the Architect take us right into the heart of the enemy's camp. What would happen to Trendon now? I only hoped the Architects would keep him alive to use as leverage. If anything happened to him, I would refuse to cooperate. They would have to kill me first.

The taxi doors opened, and several hands pulled us apart. My face felt wet and sticky from crying, but I wiped my eyes clean with the back of my hand and kept my focus on Trendon. He watched me from behind the taxi, and then I lost sight of him as the Architects carried me into the house.

With my wrists and ankles tied to the arms and legs of an uncomfortable wooden chair, I sat alone in a hollowed-out room. There were no other pieces of furniture, just my chair and the closed door in front of me. I thought about Trendon and wondered what they were doing to him at that very moment. If they caused even the slightest amount of harm to him, I would never forgive myself. I struggled against the bindings, but it was no use. They were just too tight.

The door opened, and someone stepped in. Immediately I could tell he wasn't an Architect. The man had darker skin and wore what looked like ragged pajamas. Dark, sunken eyes looked down at me in the chair as the man smiled warmly.

"Cabarles?" I asked.

"In the flesh," the Filipino answered. "Well, what's left of me anyway."

"Why are you here?" I hadn't spoken to Cabarles in months, but seeing him alive brought me hope.

"I really don't know. I haven't been out of my room in quite some time. It felt good to stretch my legs."

"Are you hurt? Have they fed you anything?" I struggled once more against the bindings.

"Hush now, Amber. Don't fret about me." Cabarles

crossed the room and took my chin in his hand. A sour smell clung to his skin, as though he hadn't bathed in months, and his hand felt hot and feverish. "It's good to see you."

"You look terrible!"

My words caused him to burst with laughter. "Well, thank you. It's good to hear a compliment. I haven't heard one in months."

"I'm serious. They can't do this to you. Where are the others? All of Dorothy's friends?"

Upon my asking this question, Cabarles's smile sobered. "I'm all that's left. Most members of the Seraphic Scroll aren't as patient as I, and Baeloc saw no need to keep them."

"He killed them?"

"They are at peace now. You mustn't worry about them. Think about yourself and nothing more."

Things were much worse than what Dorothy had known. All of her friends, with the exception of Cabarles, were dead.

"We've got to get you out of here. They have Trendon too," I said quickly, not sure of how much time we would have to speak alone. "And Dorothy has no idea where we—"

Cabarles held his finger to his lips and blinked his eyes knowingly. "Beyond your control, my dear. Do not worry about what goes on now outside of this room. I have a powerful feeling in my bones that all will turn out right."

Something had happened to Cabarles while

imprisoned in Baeloc's fortress. He had always been wise and calm, but now he seemed much different. It felt almost as though he had given up completely and had resigned himself to the fact he could do nothing to change what was bound to happen.

The door opened once more, and four members of the Qedet walked in. One of them carried a chair, which he placed on the floor in front of me while the others seized Cabarles in their arms. As they pulled him away, the Filipino smiled and gave me a supportive wink.

Like so many times before, Baeloc wore a brightly colored suit with flashy red lapels, opened to reveal his bare chest. The leader of the Architects sat in the chair in front of me and stared at me with eager eyes.

"Where's Trendon?" I demanded, glaring at the monster. I wanted so badly to free my hands and attack him, but his presence caused what little confidence I had to vanish.

Baeloc wagged his index finger and then, using an elegant feathered quill, he wrote a message on a piece of thick parchment paper before handing it to Cabarles.

"Ah, the mystery has been solved," Cabarles said, taking the paper in his hand and bowing respectfully. "I am to be your mouthpiece. How fitting."

One of the Architects holding Cabarles's arms made an awful clucking noise with his throat and shoved the Filipino in the back. Cabarles held up his hands submissively and began to read while Baeloc continued to write his next message.

Destiny has brought you here tonight, Ms. Rawson. I thank

you in advance for the role you will play in fulfilling this legacy. In a few moments, I shall take you to the grave, and with the Source, you shall summon the Shomehr to bring forth the Fire.

I blinked in confusion. The Source? The Shomehr? What was he talking about?

"I don't understand. You want me to do what?" I asked.

"The Source is what they call the Tebah Stick," Cabarles explained.

"So what are the Shomehr?"

Baeloc only stared at me as he passed the next instruction to Cabarles.

You shall do exactly as told. Deviate from my instruction and your friend will die. The Shomehr are not to approach any of my people. If I feel threatened, I will kill Trendon. We know there are six Shomehr. Do not try to deceive us.

There was that word again. Shomehr. That must be the name of the creatures from the cave. I had never heard them referred to as that, but clearly, Baeloc understood the dangers of allowing me access to the Tebah Stick. He wouldn't have forgotten what I had commanded the creatures to do back in the Philippines. Two of his men along with Malcolm, Jasher's bodyguard, had died at the hands of the Shomehr. They were far more powerful than any of Baeloc's Architects.

"And if I do exactly as you say, will you let us go? All of us, including Cabarles and the rest of Dorothy's friends?" Baeloc had already begun his next message when I blurted out my question. He paused, scribbled out some words, and wrote a quick response.

Cabarles smiled grimly. "He says, 'No, you will not be let go.' Not too shocking, if you ask me."

"Then I won't help." I clamped my mouth shut tight, grinding my molars together. The answer seemed simple. If I didn't do as they asked, they would kill Trendon and eventually me. But if I did, they would still kill us both and I would have helped them gain control over the artifact. It was a lose-lose situation. What was the point of playing fair?

Baeloc grinned, and his thin lips pulled back, revealing yellow teeth. I couldn't keep myself from shuddering. This time, he wrote a full page worth of words.

You will be obedient. If you try to resist, I will kill Trendon and then I will send my men to Dorothy's compound in Amman and burn it to the ground with everyone inside. I will then go to Gelding to visit your parents and also to Washburn Lake to visit Trendon's family. I will take my time with them. Is that what you want?

A couple of tears slid down my cheek. "No," I whispered. "Please don't do that. I'll do as you ask."

Baeloc's smile widened as he wrote his final response.

Very good, Amber Rawson. You are wise not to defy me.

He stood, and the Architects untied my bindings and surrounded me as I followed Baeloc out of the room.

"Remember, Amber, be brave," Cabarles whispered from behind me. "Do as they tell you, and this will all work out in the end." His voice trailed off, and I closed my eyes, wondering what would become of him.

19

Approximately three miles northeast of Baeloc's fortress, the Orontes River branched into two separate arms. At the point of the fork, the river's current increased in speed, but just before it split, the waters became as still as plate glass. Thickets of thistle bushes and pomegranate trees sprouted up from the banks. It was all very peaceful and serene, as though the image could've been used on a postcard. On the western bank of the river, about a hundred yards across, several goats grazed in the taller grasses as the procession of vehicles came to a stop. The back door of the SUV opened, and Baeloc escorted me to a small, abandoned church surrounded by fig and olive trees. The area near the church had been excavated, with wooden scaffolding descending more than thirty feet into the ground. A strong spotlight shone into the hole, and the top rungs of a ladder rested against the edge. More Architects piled out of the other SUVs and surrounded me.

The spotlight easily illuminated the stone outline of

what appeared to be a tomb at the bottom of the hole. The cover had been removed, but the sepulchre looked empty.

"Is that it?" I asked. "Is that Elisha's grave?"

Baeloc nodded and handed me a message.

Climb down.

"You want me to climb down there?" My voice rose apprehensively.

Baeloc grabbed my arm and directed me to the ladder.

I descended alone into the hole, with the sound of my pulse pounding in my ears. I wondered what I would find once I arrived at the bottom. Stories of the two Biblical prophets spun through my mind. They were not men to be disrespected, and if that was indeed the final resting place of Elisha, I shouldn't be down there disrupting its solitude.

When my feet touched the bottom, I looked up. The spotlight shone like a sun behind Baeloc as the other Architects gathered around him. His eyes were darker now, and I could no longer make out their color. I stood for several moments, unsure of my next move. At no more than ten feet in diameter, the hole felt crowded and damp. The ground surrounding the tomb had only been removed just beneath its opening, giving me full access to stare into the bottom. The stone looked like granite, and several Hebraic characters had been inscribed around the edges. A white powdery substance coated the walls, and I wondered if they were calcium deposits from the decomposed remains of Elisha. I didn't want to think about it. Standing in the frightening dark of the grave, all I wanted to do was find the artifact and be done with it.

"What am I supposed to do?" I finally asked after finding the courage to speak.

One of the Architects lowered a wooden container into the hole with a rope. Baeloc had taped yet another piece of instruction to the box.

Remember the lives of your friends and your family rests with your actions. Do not try anything with the Shomehr.

I opened the box and swallowed.

The Tebah Stick seemed smaller than I remembered. The polished blue stone at its crown was no bigger than a grapefruit, and the wooden handle, glittering with red jewels, stretched no longer than my forearm. Reaching in, my hand faltered just before closing around the handle.

"Come on, Amber," I whispered to myself. "You can do this." I closed my eyes and squeezed my fingers, immediately sensing the power contained within the scepter.

I wanted to control it. Control *them*. And I knew the creatures were close by. Electricity crackled through me, and up above, I could feel the Shomehr emerging from the shadows of the trees and surrounding the Architects. I didn't look up but kept my eyes focused on the artifact.

Suddenly Baeloc shouted, growling in his foreign tongue. I couldn't understand the words, but I didn't need to read any handwritten messages to know they were threats. He was afraid of what I might command, and for good reason. Already I had shared my thoughts with the creatures, and they had readied themselves to obey. They could do it quickly. There were six of them in the woods, and they were much stronger and faster than Baeloc's men could ever dream of being. All I had to do was state my command and they would kill everyone above the grave. Why take any more chances? I was tired of being scared of Baeloc, and they would eliminate that problem.

Baeloc screamed now in desperation. I looked upward, and my heartbeat quickened. I felt another push of urgency from the creatures. They desperately wanted to act and seemed to whisper in my head.

Give the command. We'll kill them all.

But that wasn't all. They believed I was an imposter. I should've never touched the Tebah Stick in the first place. They obeyed simply because of the power exuding from the artifact, and if given the chance, they would fall upon me like the others.

I regained control of my mind and blocked out their voices. Did I really want them to kill everyone? Was that my idea, or had it come from the creatures? Realizing I shouldn't take any more risks, I retrained my focus on the tomb.

"Show it to me," I whispered. "Show me the artifact." I squeezed the Tebah Stick in my hands and waited for the creatures to obey my command. Instead, I felt as though the creatures resisted me. I could sense them withdrawing from the church and could almost see their movements in my mind.

"The artifact!" I repeated. "I want you to find it."

But the Shomehr seemed distant now. I wasn't sure

exactly what to expect, but I just assumed the creatures would join me in the tomb. Was Elijah's Fire not down here? Maybe Baeloc had made a mistake. Maybe this wasn't the burial site of Elisha. How could he be certain? No other archaeologist had ever stumbled upon it in thousands of years.

After a while, I heard footsteps on the ladder, but they didn't belong to one of the creatures. Instead, the cold hand of an Architect closed around the back of my neck. He pointed to a message and forced my head forward to read it.

Do as you're told! Do you want to see Trendon killed?

Upon reading this, I dropped the Tebah Stick, and it clattered along the edge of the sepulchre before dropping to the dirt floor. Immediately, my connection with the creatures ended, and I expelled a deep, gasping breath. The Architect released his hold on my neck and scrambled to collect the artifact.

"I tried!" I shouted, still gulping breaths of air. "They wouldn't listen!"

With the Architect behind me, I ascended the ladder to ground level. Baeloc glared at me as he tensely scribbled his next command.

You are to try again. Do I need to prove to you what I am capable of doing?

With the snap of his fingers, the door of one of the vehicles opened, and the Architects pulled Cabarles from the back.

"No!" I shouted. "Leave him alone! I swear I tried!"

Cabarles stood before me, smiling and nodding

softly. "There, there, Amber. Be at peace," he whispered. Baeloc held his hand out, and another Architect pressed a gun into his palm.

"No wait! I'll try again! Give it to me! I promise you I'll try." I wiggled my fingers, demanding the Tebah Stick, and Baeloc handed me the artifact. The wave of energy returned, surging through my veins and filling my chest with power. But the creatures were leaving me, leaving the grave site.

"They're going away," I said, staring at Baeloc. "I don't think they'll listen to me. I'm trying! What do I tell them?"

Baeloc cocked the gun and pointed it at Cabarles's chest.

"Calm yourself, Amber." Cabarles bowed his head, awaiting his death. "All will be well."

"Please!" I begged the creatures in my mind. "Help me!" I pleaded with them to come back, but they weren't listening. What did I need to say to earn their allegiance? Over and over, I called to them with my thoughts, but nothing happened.

Baeloc's eyes sparkled as he pulled the trigger.

Click.

I screamed and collapsed to my knees, unwilling to look at the devastation.

"It is okay, Amber. I'm still here." The Architects released Cabarles, and he fell to the ground with me, swooping me up in his arms. I sobbed out of control but still clung to the Tebah Stick in my hands. "It's all an act," he whispered soothingly. "They didn't shoot me. I'm fine. Look for yourself."

Looking at Cabarles's chest, I searched for the blood and the bullet hole but realized the gun had never gone off. It hadn't been loaded. Several of the Architects produced chilling sounds, which I believed to be their form of laughter. I allowed the Tebah Stick to fall from my fingertips, and then I passed out in Cabarles's arms.

20

I slept and dreamt of Abelish lying in a coffin. In my dream, Abelish had died destroying the artifact. He had looked peaceful, as though only asleep, but the painful marks of his disease seemed to glow on his skin. Dorothy had attended the funeral, as did Trendon and Lisa. Other than the four of us, not one person had paid their respects. I could remember crying in my dream, but none of us spoke.

When I awoke, eleven hours later, my eyes opened to grime-covered walls with faded and peeling wallpaper. The room smelled horrendous, old and decayed like a family of rats had nested beneath the floorboards. Beneath me, a threadbare mattress with awkward springs squealed as I sat up, blinking away the sleep from my eyes.

"I've been instructed to tell you they will be here soon to have you try again."

I turned to see Cabarles seated on a stool in the corner by a flickering lamp.

"I thought they shot you!" I rushed over to him and threw my arms around his neck.

"I did too!" he said as he patted my back. "Alas, I'm still here."

"Where's here? What is this place?"

"We're back at Baeloc's home on the main level. I believe my room is just seven rooms that way." He pointed toward the wall. "Quaint, isn't it?"

"Do you know where they're keeping Trendon?"

He shook his head. "I'm afraid not. I've been here with you the whole time."

I once again sat on the cot and rubbed my eyes. "The Tebah Stick didn't work. I tried to make the creatures help me, but they didn't listen." Cabarles held his hands in his lap but didn't say anything. "I don't understand. At first, I could hear them in my head. They wanted to obey me, but I had to command them. It's as though they couldn't act on their own and needed my words to tell them what to do. Why do you think that is?"

Curling his lower lip thoughtfully, Cabarles raised an eyebrow. "I cannot tell you. I don't know much about the artifact."

"But you were a Sentry over it. You guarded it."

"From a distance, Amber. I never went as far into the mountain as you and Trendon. But I will say this. My people of Arayat sleep peacefully now since your visit. The wailing no longer keeps them up at night."

"Well, I guess that's a good thing."

"Of course it is. You protected the artifact, and I suppose you released those creatures . . ."

"The Shomehr," I said.

Cabarles smiled. "Yes, that's what the Architects call them. It's a Hebraic word for *Guardian*. I'm not sure if that's their true name or not. But that's what Baeloc calls them. Nevertheless, you did a good thing when you released them."

"But they're here now, and I think they're waiting for me."

Cabarles nodded. "It would appear you are in control of their actions."

"But that wasn't the case when we were in the mountain. Those things attacked us, and one of them slashed Trendon's chest! They were trying to kill us. Why did they change all of a sudden?"

Cabarles looked down and pondered my question. "Maybe before, they were under the control of the Tebah Stick's previous owner. They had been given one charge, which was to protect the artifact, and they could do whatever was necessary to make sure it never fell into the hands of an enemy. When you and Trendon came along and you took control of the Tebah Stick, maybe that changed things for them. You became their master."

I rubbed the tender area around my shoulder, feeling the bump where the glass had been. Had that really happened over a week ago? "Okay, if I really do control them, why didn't they listen?"

"What were you asking them to do?" Cabarles asked.

"I wanted them to show me the artifact."

"Were you specific about which artifact you wanted? There are many powerful ones in the world."

"I didn't need to be specific. They were in my head and knew what I wanted." I remembered the voices of the creatures sounding in my mind. We had been connected for a short period of time. They knew my thoughts and understood exactly my commands.

Cabarles fidgeted with his collar, and the fabric flapped open for a moment, revealing his withered chest. I could see the distinct shape of his ribs beneath his thin, starved skin. Baeloc had been withholding food from him. Starving him. How long had that gone on? "And then what did they do?" Cabarles asked.

"They left." I sighed. "They went away." The memory of their disobedience still frustrated me. Because they refused to listen, I almost saw Cabarles murdered.

"Just like that? Up and left?" Cabarles tapped his index finger against his lips. "Why do you think that is?"

"I don't know. I must've said the wrong things or given the wrong commands."

"Perhaps." He nodded. "Or maybe it's not as you think. Maybe they weren't really leaving you, they were just . . ." His voice trailed off.

"What?" I asked.

"I don't dare guess, Amber. I'm not the one in charge, and I would not want to be the reason for leading you astray. But . . ." He stood and joined me on the cot. "It would seem if these creatures were at your command and you desired their help to find Elijah's Fire, then they wouldn't just abandon you to find it on your own."

"But that's what they did!" I ran my hand through my hair.

"You need to be at peace, Amber. It will come to you, and you will know what to do."

"That's not all of it, Cabarles." I sighed and stared at my hands. "The creatures spoke to me in my mind and wanted me to release them. They wanted to kill Baeloc and all of my enemies." I looked up, my lips trembling. "I almost did. It would've been easy. I could've had them kill every one of the Architects. It really scared me."

"But you didn't, Amber."

"Should I have? Wouldn't that have been the best thing?"

Cabarles smiled. "No, that would've been terrible. You are better than that. You are brilliant and kind. Killing Baeloc may be what needs to happen in the end, but that won't make it easy. And certainly a fifteen-year-old girl has no business delivering that sort of judgment. Promise me that whatever happens, you won't let your mind wander. Baeloc will have you try again tonight, and you must let your fears go, but don't let your guard down. Don't listen to the Shomehr. Control them. Do not let them control you."

I sighed deeply but then nodded. "All right. But I won't let anything happen to you or Trendon if I can help it."

I wanted to see Trendon. I wanted to run my fingers through his curly hair and punch him in the stomach for not running when I told him to. Cabarles seemed to have an iron will when it came to starvation, but Trendon wouldn't last even a few hours without snacks. This needed to end.

"Cabarles?" I asked. "What's this thing I'm looking for? How will I know for sure if I've found it?"

"In the time I've been here, I've observed much," Cabarles said, leaning close and whispering in my ear. "Though I've yet to understand their hideous language, I have picked up on a few subtle clues. Elijah's Fire, as you know, was a weapon the prophet used to call fire down from heaven. He considered it a prized possession and passed it on to Elisha." I remembered all of that from my discussions with Dorothy. "Unlike the nature of Elijah, who used loud and convincing means of showing his power, the artifact itself was far more subtle and may have had a more practical use before it became so destructive."

"Practical use? What was it used for?"

"Baeloc believes the prophet Elijah once used the artifact for woodcutting."

"Like an ax?"

"Exactly, Amber. An ax would've been simple and small—something Elijah could've easily kept hidden on his person."

I had imagined Elijah's Fire to be more like the Tebah Stick: a scepter or a staff. "Do you believe that?" I asked.

"Your guess is as good as mine," Cabarles whispered. "But I will say this about our gracious host. Baeloc has unusual means of discovering what no archaeologist could do in thousands of years. He has sources unlike any Dorothy has ever used. So I would venture to say, he may be somewhat accurate in that description."

"What sources does he have?" So many questions.

So little time to truly dwell on them. It was good to have Cabarles here to bounce ideas off of, but I knew it wouldn't last much longer.

"Let us not talk of such things."

But I wasn't ready to kill the conversation just yet. Not with Baeloc somewhere outside of my room, preparing to pounce on me at the right moment. I was on the verge of assisting him in his evil plot, and I needed to know what I was to do. Cabarles may have been broken and ready to allow fate to work its way through this mess, but I wasn't.

"What do I do once I find the ax? Do I give it to Baeloc? Wouldn't that be the end of everything?"

Cabarles shook his head. "Not the end." He clicked his tongue and tilted his head, looking at me with his friendly eyes. "Baeloc is evil, and he's motivated by hatred. Because of that motivation, people will suffer, and it may seem as though all will be lost. But you have to remember one important rule. Where there's evil, there's also good. If you allow yourself to believe, miracles can happen for you."

"Have you seen miracles?" I asked.

Cabarles nodded. "I have. But those are mine to keep secret. Just believe, Amber, in a greater power. Because it exists. And no matter how terrible things get, you need to think about what our friend Elisha once said many years ago." I shook my head, not knowing the answer, and Cabarles squeezed my hand. "*Fear not. For they that be with us are more than they that be with them.*"

Warmth grew inside of me, filling my body with courage and peace as we sat together in silence.

The door opened, and Baeloc entered. He pointed at Cabarles, and I watched the Architects take him away, hopefully back to his cell and nothing worse. Baeloc then nodded at me and held out his hand as an invitation to join him in the hallway.

21

Unlike Dorothy's compound, where there were rooms on multiple floors, Baeloc's fortress contained all of the lodgings on the ground level. A hallway with tattered carpet and wooden floorboards that groaned beneath every step stretched past nearly fifteen closed doors. Chandeliers covered with flaccid cobwebs hung from the ceiling, with all but a few of their lightbulbs burned out. The remaining light failed to brighten the surroundings and instead cast thick shadows beyond the carpet's edge, making everything feel like a dungeon. The hall seemed unnaturally quiet as I listened for any sounds of life beyond each door we passed.

At last we arrived at the final door before the hallway ended at a wall and another side hall joined it to the right. Baeloc opened the door, and I caught myself from shouting for joy.

Trendon sat cross-legged in the corner of an even darker room, squinting toward the light.

"Trendon!" I said, but when I started to run to him, the Architects held me back.

"Hey, Amber," Trendon grumbled. "Are you done yet? This is pretty boring." He stood but didn't come any closer. That was when I noticed the steel shackle clamping his leg to a post in the floor. They had chained him up like a dog so he couldn't even walk around the room! What kind of cruel people did that to a fifteen-year-old kid? Trendon noticed me gawking at his chain.

"Oh yeah, that?" he said, smiling proudly at his ankle. "I deserved that. I'm actually very happy about it, so don't worry."

"What did you do?" I asked, still appalled at the sight of his condition.

"If you see a guy walking around here with really pale skin and growling like a . . . wait a minute, they all do that. Never mind. Let's just say, one of these bozos will be looking cross-eyed for quite some time after I hit him with a stick." Trendon glared defiantly at Baeloc.

"Have you been treated okay?" I asked. There were no beds. No chairs or furniture, and no light whatsoever. Of course he hadn't been treated okay. These were worse than prison conditions.

"This place sucks!" he spat. "But, oh well. What can you do?" He sat back down on the floor and fiddled with the chain at his ankle. "How about you? Are you still sleeping in luxury?"

"It's better than this."

"Why am I not surprised? How about Elijah's Fire? You found it yet so we can go home?"

Before I could answer, Baeloc pulled me out of the room and slammed the door. I could hear Trendon shouting some obscenities in the corner, but Baeloc ignored it and handed me a message.

Now that you see what I've done to him, do you believe I'll do worse? Because I will, Amber. Time is running out for your friends, all of them. I want the artifact.

"I know you want it!" I wadded up the paper and tossed it back at him. "And I want to give it to you, but it didn't work. I held the Tebah Stick, and I commanded the creatures to listen, but it was as though they couldn't hear me. Maybe if you told me what to do . . ." I groaned in aggravation. "And why do you want it so bad? You have the Tebah Stick, and it doesn't work for you. Why do you think Elijah's Fire will be any different?" Baeloc's eyes barely blinked, but he made no attempt to respond. "You're pathetic! Are you that desperate for power? I know you've lived a sad life, but that doesn't mean you have to punish everyone else. Why not just go away and leave us alone? We've suffered enough!" I felt I had said too much, but my anger could not be restrained. Baeloc watched me for several moments before writing once more.

Suffered? You know nothing of suffering. My people have lived for generations with suffering. And now I intend to end it forever.

I read the passage and for a brief moment actually felt sorry for Baeloc and the Architects. I supposed they *had* lived their lives with suffering. But then I shook the thought from my mind. Suffering didn't make it right for them to kill and torture others.

"I don't understand how this artifact will end your suffering. What are you going to use it for?"

Revenge.

That one word on the page told enough of the story, but Baeloc wasn't finished there. Leading me through the mansion, we stepped out into the expansive yard behind the building. The sun had begun to descend. I had no idea what time it was, but I figured it to be sometime in the early afternoon. The dead grass crunched beneath our feet as we walked briskly away from the house. Baeloc's Architects followed us eagerly, crowding close to me as we walked.

When I first saw it, I didn't know how to react, and my mind struggled to process the sight. The yard sloped downward toward the river, which explained why I never saw it when we first arrived at Baeloc's fortress. At the base of the hill, the Architects had constructed a monstrous tower along the banks of the Orontes River.

The Tower of Babel.

I knew immediately upon seeing it what it was. The tower stood several stories tall and was constructed mostly of wooden timbers and mud. A square, wooden platform had been built at the top of the tower with a stone podium at its center. Apparently Baeloc and the Architects were eager to enter heaven.

"Are you kidding me? Is that what I think it is?" I almost laughed at the ridiculous sight. Why would he ever think he could use that to enter heaven? The Architects were clearly delusional. Even if they had an endless supply of wood and manpower to construct a tower, they would never have enough to reach above the tallest mountains, let alone all the way to heaven.

And didn't they remember what had happened to their ancestors? That didn't work out for them. Were they just destined to follow the same path as before?

"Why are you building another Tower of Babel?" I asked. I actually felt anger upon seeing the tower. It meant all of the fear and suffering my friends and I had endured had happened because of a stupid man's fantasy.

Baeloc threw his head back and laughed. Though it didn't sound like laughter. More like the cackle of a hyena. The sick choking sound shook his whole body, and his minions followed suit, joining Baeloc with laughter. I covered my ears and cringed at the sound, hoping it would end soon. But Baeloc and the Architects continued to fill the air with their gut-churning voices. It took several minutes to calm his laughter, but then Baeloc wrote his response.

That is not the Tower of Babel. That is the Tower of Despar, the original architect. And the tower was never meant to reach heaven in the first place. Why would we ever want to go there?

His words confused me. "Then what's it for?"

Baeloc smiled at several of his Architects as their laughter died off. They were a brotherhood of evil, united in one purpose, but I had yet to discover what that was. Baeloc returned his gaze to me and tilted his head as if considering whether or not he deemed me worthy to know his vision. Then he answered my question.

The Tower of Despar is only a vessel to harness the full power of the Weapons of Might. With all three artifacts combined, the tower will channel its energy and release a cataclysmic explosion. One that would permanently end mankind forever.

I reread the note three times, making sure I understood. How could he do that? Could the tower truly harness the power of the artifacts and explode? A few months ago I would've never believed such a power existed, but my opinions had changed from what I had experienced. Anything was possible.

"Why would you do that?" I gasped. "Destroy mankind? You would die too! All of you."

That would be a necessary sacrifice. One we have all vowed to make to fulfill our destiny. Revenge is what we're after.

I scanned the faces of the Architects, searching for any signs of doubt. Joseph and Sherez had told me there were others who no longer agreed with Baeloc and were willing to rebel against him. Were they still there?

"This is crazy!" I shouted. "Listen to him! He wants to destroy everyone, including you. Is that what you really want?"

More cackling laughter erupted from the ranks of the Architects. Their chests heaved as they found great humor in my words. Apparently all of the rebels had left or even been killed, and only the hardened followers of Baeloc remained. It certainly appeared I had no allies and was utterly alone.

22

Midnight.

I sat on my cot, my bare feet grazing the floor, as I listened to something scampering in the walls. The soft patter of its paws ran along the floorboards, and I wondered whether it was a rat or a really big cockroach. Outside, rain peppered the mansion walls. I had seen the clouds earlier, but the rain only began a few minutes ago.

I had endured another exhausting three hours of failure. Baeloc had once again taken me to Elisha's grave, but the Shomehr had refused to listen to me. In fact, they never showed up at the burial site. I tried to remember the way my mind had worked the first time I controlled them, in the Philippines. The creatures had responded instantly to my commands. I had felt at one with them, and a thought needed only to register in my head for them to act. Something had changed since then. The Shomehr had grown stubborn and unwilling to cooperate.

Baeloc's patience had been all but spent. Tomorrow, he would have me try for the last time before resorting to violence, and Cabarles would be his victim. That had been Baeloc's threat, and from the way he had glowered at me when he'd shoved me back into his vehicle and we'd pulled away from the burial site, I believed he wouldn't hesitate to go through with it.

I just couldn't understand why the Tebah Stick wouldn't work. No matter what I asked, the creatures never obeyed. Was there some sort of secret password or ritual I needed to perform to gain their allegiance? And if so, how would I ever find out what to do? It wasn't like I could research the topic. Even if Baeloc had provided me with reading materials, where would I begin? Maybe there was a book out there containing the correct procedures for controlling the Shomehr, but I seriously doubted it.

Complete silence had settled in the hallways. If there were Architects patrolling outside my door, then they moved like ghosts. My stomach grumbled, and I longed for a bite to eat. I remembered the Halloumi Salad and the Mansaf Abelish had served us back at Dorothy's compound. I could almost taste the olives. At least Baeloc had given me water, but the liquid sloshing around in the clay jug on the floor next to my cot definitely didn't taste like water. Then my thoughts turned to Trendon. How hungry was he? Starving? Had the Architects offered him any sort of sustenance? I couldn't believe they would. Not when they intended to use him as a means of leverage. Baeloc must have understood my feelings for Trendon and therefore assumed seeing him suffer would force me to control the creatures. If that were only the case, I would gladly do anything just to know Trendon had been given some food. But the Tebah Stick didn't work that way.

Suddenly the lock on my door unlatched. I turned and watched as the doorknob jiggled. Just great. Baeloc wasn't going to wait until tomorrow. It would end tonight. I hugged my arms and waited for him to enter, wondering if he would drag Cabarles or Trendon into my room to prove his point. But the door moved only a crack and never opened any wider.

Slowly, I leaned forward on my cot and pressed my hands against the mattress. Was this more theatrics? Would Baeloc wait for me to stand before he threw open the door and seized me? Resting my feet against the floor, I hesitantly pushed up with my hands off the cot.

"Hello?" I whispered. "What do you want?" They had me as their prisoner. I couldn't go anywhere, and Dorothy had no way of knowing where we were, so they really didn't need to rush. Baeloc's impatience to end human life disgusted me. When no response came, I quietly crossed the room and gripped the doorknob. Part of me feared to open it, thinking an Architect would jump out at me at any moment. Then I began to wonder if Cabarles or Trendon had somehow managed to escape their rooms and were waiting for me to sneak out with them.

Closing my eyes, I held my breath and pulled the door open. The wood made an awful creaking sound as the ancient hinges protested against the action. It echoed throughout my room, and I bit my lower lip, cringing from the sound.

The hallway directly in front of my door stood empty. But not entirely empty. There seemed to be a haze gathered in the air, carrying a musty scent like the faint smell of a wet animal. I felt the unpleasant sensation of prickling skin rising on my arms and shoulders as I cautiously stepped through the doorway and peered down the hall. At first I didn't recognize the figure standing down at the other end staring at me through the mist. But then I caught myself before I screamed.

One of the Shomehr stood just beyond Trendon's room. Its yellow eyes pierced the thick fog gathered around its body. Like before, I couldn't make out the monster's features, just its eyes and the outline of its frightening body, which easily towered above six feet in height. I didn't move or breathe. I wanted to jump back in the room and slam the door, but I had frozen at the sight of the creature. After a few moments of watching me, it turned and disappeared down the side hallway.

Finally I clutched my chest, gasping for air. That monster had just opened my door! I stepped back into my room, hating to be alone, but before I latched the door shut, I stopped and pulled it back open. By the way the creature had stood patiently at the end of the hallway, waiting for me to come out before it walked away, I knew it wanted me to follow it.

Without taking time to think things through, I hurriedly slipped on my shoes and crept out of my room. Upon arriving by Trendon's door, I considered opening it to help him but remembered the steel clamp around his ankle with no means of removing it. Staring back down the way I came, I looked for Cabarles's door. He had told me his room had been seven doors down from mine, but I didn't know which side. I couldn't stall any longer and would have to follow the creature on my own.

As I had expected, the Shomehr still waited for me, though it retreated down to the end of the side hallway and stood in the foyer. Wet footprints lined the floor leading up to the creature. Though longer and wider than normal footprints, their shape could have easily come from a man. I took several cautious steps toward the creature but realized it seemed too quiet in the mansion. How was I able to simply walk down the hallway, unseen by any of the Architects?

The answer came almost immediately. Lying on the ground at the creature's feet were the bodies of two Architects. They must have been standing guard when the Shomehr unexpectedly pounced on them. Though they had guns, it didn't matter against the monsters. I caught a whimper in my throat as a feeling of light-headedness nearly caused my knees to buckle.

"I can't do this," I said in an undertone as the Shomehr left the mansion through the main entry doors. I didn't want to look at the dead bodies on the ground, but my eyes kept returning to them. Suddenly, the confinement of my room and my starvation didn't seem like bad ideas anymore, considering the alternative. Was I actually going to follow the creature out of the building? Then I remembered what Cabarles had told me. I was in charge. No matter what, the Shomehr would listen to me. But then I realized I didn't have the Tebah Stick in my possession, and I panicked. How could I control them without it? They couldn't read my thoughts, and I had no way of knowing their intentions. This was absolutely crazy! Once again, my eyes fell upon the bodies of the Architects. That creature could do so much worse, and there were still five more of them. But if they'd wanted to, I would've been killed in my room. Instead, the Shomehr let me out. If they hadn't killed me yet, it had to mean they were trying to help me. Maybe. Or maybe they wanted to eat me outside of the mansion.

Regardless of my fear and the unknown of what lay in wait, I stepped out onto the lawn and followed the creature into the woods.

23

Like the skeletal remains of a recently extinguished burned building, the wooden scaffolding covering Elisha's grave glistened with water. The rain had ceased its downpour, but sporadic drops continued to fall as the clouds slowly dispersed, revealing the thumbnail of the moon. The journey to the church had taken more than an hour but had gone without confrontation. No one seemed to follow us, but I knew it would be only a matter of time before Baeloc learned of what had happened. Dead bodies usually provided ample proof. But I couldn't worry about that anymore. I had other concerns on my mind.

With the spotlight turned off, an almost suffocating darkness had gathered around the excavation site, and the hole leading down to the grave resembled the outline of an old well. There would be a substantial amount of water inside the tomb. The ladder rungs would be slick, and without means of illumination, the descent would be treacherous. I didn't want to climb down there, not with that thing lurking close by, and I began to imagine horrible thoughts of Elisha's body appearing at the bottom of the ladder, trying to get to me.

"Stop it, Amber!" I hissed under my breath. Those types of thoughts would only cripple me. I hoped I wouldn't need to climb down there, but the creature only paused briefly near the hole before continuing on toward the river. Where was it going? Too afraid to ask it outright, I followed for another half mile before the Shomehr finally stopped at a point where the river widened considerably. The smooth water reflected the smiling moon above, but then it rippled as the creature broke the surface and stepped into the river.

Suddenly there were more of them. Five other heads emerged from the river, dark and wet. Once in the water, the haze vanished. Though I couldn't see the creatures perfectly, I could make out one alarming trait. The Shomehr had smooth skin and almost human-like faces. I supposed I had expected to see fur-covered features like that of a wolf or some other sort of animal, but I had been wrong. Their eyes still glowed despite the darkness as they stared at me standing on the bank.

Why did they bring me here? But I knew the answer. This was where they had gone when I first ordered them to find me the artifact. They hadn't disobeyed; I just never understood, which meant the burial site was not the location of Elijah's Fire. But why were they helping me now? I didn't have the Tebah Stick in my possession, and I'd never connected with them before without it. Only in a dream.

My dreams! Had they been premonitions all along? Would I find a wet cave beneath the water? And in that cave, would I find Elijah's ax?

Another memory rushed into my mind. I remembered reading about one particular miracle in the second book of Kings where Elisha had made an ax float to the top of a river. At the time I had questioned the significance of that event. Why had the prophet used his power to do that? It seemed unnecessary. Dropping the ax in the water had been an accident, but the man who had done it had acted fearful because the ax never belonged to him. He had borrowed it from someone else, thinking he could use it to cut down the trees. I then began to realize from whom he had borrowed it.

The Shomehr still floated in the water, staring at me as if waiting for my next move. Kicking off my shoes, I rolled up my pant legs and stepped into the river. Like ice, the water instantly chilled my blood, and my teeth began to chatter. All at once the Shomehr dove. With no time to change my mind, I filled my lungs with air and dove headfirst as well.

I was swimming in ink. The black water yielded zero light, and I had no way of knowing in which direction my strokes took me. The pull against my body to return to the surface acted as the only bearing. I couldn't hold my breath for more than a minute, and before I had swum ten feet down, my lungs had began to ache. Just a few more feet and then I would stop. If at that point I hadn't found the bottom, I would have no choice but to go up for air. But there seemed to be no end of it, and without being able to see even a few inches in front of my face, I decided to surrender.

Suddenly, a small blue light pierced the blackness as my necklace started to glow. The locator stone could be used to find secret entryways leading to artifacts. It had worked before in the Philippines, and like the Tebah Stick, someone had marked the location of Elijah's Fire using similar means. But I didn't know how much farther I needed to swim, and my chest burned with a longing for air.

Turning upward, I kicked furiously against the current but found my way blocked as something swam in front of me. I pushed against its body and realized one of the Shomehr was preventing me from swimming back to the surface. Air bubbles flowed out of my mouth as I tried to slide past, my lungs blazing with pain and my hands fiercely slapping within the water. What was it doing? Why was it stopping me? Couldn't it understand I needed air? Just a quick breath! I struggled furiously, my eyes clamping tight as I inwardly begged for the surface. Then the creature's claws closed around my arms and I drifted out of consciousness.

Retching, I vomited awful-tasting water onto the floor of some cave as I sucked in air until the pain in my lungs finally eased. I didn't know whether I was below the riverbed or had been taken into a hole beneath the shoreline. At the moment, I didn't care. I thought I had drowned, but the Shomehr must have saved me and brought me to the cave.

Freezing, I hugged my knees against my chest as my sopping wet clothes dripped puddles on the floor. I looked for signs of the creatures, but they had gone. The cave was more like a grotto and no bigger than a small room, with a low ceiling of stalactites and a dark pool of water providing the only entrance. The locator stone in my necklace still glowed brilliantly, and along the edge of the pool, some of the stones glowed as well, filling the room with an eerie blue light. Once again, Dorothy's gift had led me to my destination.

Something in the corner of the grotto caught my eye, and I discovered a stone box almost camouflaged by the surrounding rocks. The box itself wasn't too heavy, and I immediately recognized the familiar pattern of lines swirling over it. Petrified wood. Thousands of years hidden within the cave had turned the wooden box to stone. Fingers trembling both from excitement and the extreme cold, I removed the lid and peered inside.

At first glance, I would've never figured the artifact to be a weapon capable of disastrous miracles. Cabarles had been right. Elijah's Fire was indeed an ax, or perhaps the word "hatchet" best described it. Knotted wood made up the handle, and the dull, steel blade bore a peculiar black design.

Scorch marks.

Elijah had used the ax to rain fire from heaven. He had burned the priests of Baal as well as scores of other soldiers. I took extra caution to not mistakenly let my skin touch the artifact, because I didn't want there to be another artifact willing to work only when I held it.

"Okay," I said, my voice echoing in the cave. "I found it. Do you want me to take it?" I waited for several minutes, listening to the water lap against the edge of the pool. "Hello?" I expected to see the face of one of the creatures appear in the pool, but the black river water barely rippled. "I'll just swim back then, if that's okay?"

After ripping a few strands of fabric from my shirt to secure the lid of the box closed, I slipped back into the freezing cold water and swam to the surface.

24

The half mile back to the burial site seemed to take forever as I walked, shivering and contemplating my next few moves. I was cold and confused. I didn't want to go back to the mansion, and I certainly didn't want to turn the artifact over to the enemy. But I couldn't just leave Trendon and Cabarles at Baeloc's mercy. I needed some advice. Dorothy would know what to do, as would Abelish and maybe even Temel, but they were hours away, probably searching in the wrong direction. If only I could somehow get a signal out to Dorothy. Baeloc had to have some means of communicating. The mansion had electricity, which meant it probably had phone lines. Maybe if I had a chance, I could use a phone or a radio to send a message to her. It was possible, but it would take time. And time was the one luxury I didn't have. Glancing down at the hatchet bulging beneath the material, I debated over another question. Could I use the artifact against Baeloc?

"What do I do?" I whispered. Following the Shomehr

into the water had pushed my nerves almost past the breaking point, but now I almost longed for their company. Even if it came from murderous, faceless creatures that smelled of wet dog. They had ultimately done as I had asked them to by helping me find Elijah's Fire. Staring off in either direction, I knew they weren't following me. They had performed their task and obeyed my command. If I wanted their help again, the solution seemed clear. I would have to take hold of the Tebah Stick once more and command them to attack. When that happened, which I knew bordered the impossible, I couldn't hold them back. It would be our lives at stake, or the Architects, and I would have to make the right choice.

"Amber, get out of here!" Trendon's voice disrupted my thoughts, and my head snapped to attention.

Baeloc stood in front of the church with over a hundred Architects gathered around him. He had turned on the spotlight and had pointed it toward the river. Trendon and Cabarles knelt on the ground at Baeloc's feet with their arms tied behind their backs.

Pointing a handgun at Trendon's head, Baeloc held up his other hand and beckoned for the artifact. It was as I had figured. Baeloc had found the dead bodies of his servants and had gathered the masses around Elisha's grave. When he didn't find me there, he waited. I wished I had traveled back to the mansion using another route. I could have found a phone and given us a chance. But that was obviously not meant to be.

"Let them go first!" I ordered.

Baeloc refused to listen. Shaking his head excitedly,

he wiggled his fingers, calling for the artifact, and cocked the barrel back on the gun.

"Burn them up or run! Don't give it to them!" Trendon shouted, and I felt my heart break. Baeloc would never let him go. He never intended to let any of us go. At least he had been honest about that, but I only wished I could bargain for Trendon's life. Staring at my best friend's determined face, I realized it wouldn't matter. Trendon would never leave me. I didn't know why I never thought about it before. Through everything, he had always been there with me. Yes, he complained and argued and drove me crazy with his rudeness, but not once did he ever abandon me. Who else could I say that about? Joseph? Dorothy? No. Each of them had left me at some point, but not him. Trendon was the greatest friend a girl could have.

My eyes fell upon Cabarles, who wore a grim look across his face. He had promised me all would turn out okay, but clearly he had not foreseen any of this happening.

Many of the Architects began to chatter in their language, and their voices rose in volume, almost chanting. I had arrived at the end of the journey and it was time to make a decision, but I had one major problem. I didn't know how to use the artifact. Would it work in a similar fashion to the Tebah Stick and use my thoughts and desires as a guide? I feared there would be more to it than that. If Baeloc sensed even a hint of my intentions, he would shoot, and this time the gun was loaded.

The chanting grew louder as I held out the stone

box and untied the bindings. I could do it. I could command the artifact and bring fire down on Baeloc. I could end everything right then, but once again I looked at Trendon. Would I have time to do all that before the gun went off? How could I hold my concentration if he died?

Baeloc's eyes widened. He looked possessed and psychotic, as if he would shoot Trendon just for the fun of it. The victory was his, and he knew it. He no longer needed to listen to my orders. My lack of confidence seemed evidence enough I wouldn't attempt to use the artifact. I only wondered why he hadn't simply aimed the gun and shot me. That would've been the easiest thing to do, but maybe Baeloc still felt uncertainty about the Shomehr.

I closed my eyes and released a deflated sigh. "Okay, you win," I said, making no attempt to open the box. "Just point the gun away from Trendon and I'll give it to you." I made my choice, and all I could do then was hope for a miracle.

After several heated seconds, Baeloc dropped the gun at his side. I didn't want to let him win, but what other choice did I have? I covered the short distance between us and surrendered the weapon into the Architect's hand.

"What are you doing?" Trendon asked, his voice sounding defeated.

All at once the air filled with an abundance of sound. Baeloc's followers joined in unison, raising their voices in celebration. The clouds thundered overhead, and I didn't know if it came from the lingering storm or if Baeloc had already begun to harness the energy of Elijah's Fire.

But something else overshadowed all of those sounds.

A deafening explosion detonated back in the direction of the mansion. The earth trembled beneath our feet, and I staggered forward, barely catching my balance. The entire multitude of Architects swiveled their heads in surprise as the night sky lit up with orange light.

"Did someone leave the oven on?" Trendon asked, cracking an awkward smile.

Baeloc's face bore a mixture of bafflement and anger. A second explosion not as powerful as the first rang out, and though I had no way of knowing for sure, I had a feeling I knew what had caused the eruption. It certainly looked like the handiwork of my sunglasses-wearing friend.

Trendon looked at me, and I knew he thought the same thing.

"Temel?" he whispered. I nodded, and his smile widened. "Oh, is it about to get thick or what?"

Disorder broke out within the ranks of the Architects. They didn't seem to know what they should be doing. Baeloc hissed his command, and several of them snatched Cabarles and Trendon from the ground and charged off toward the row of vehicles parked beyond the church.

"Wait!" I shouted. "Where are you taking them?"

Baeloc ignored me as six of the SUVs, one of them carrying Trendon and Cabarles, raced away from the site, spinning dirt and rocks in their wake. I had no time to worry about them. At least for now they were safe and away from Baeloc's itchy trigger finger. Baeloc barked other orders to the remaining Architects, and though his voice bore no semblance to any common language I had ever heard, his growling possessed an excited and nervous tone to it. Everyone chattered back and forth, nodding their heads, as they understood what was expected of them. But then the voices died off as something new appeared, demanding their full attention.

Dorothy and Abelish stepped out from behind the church, and my mouth dropped open.

"What are you doing here?" I screamed. How in the world did they ever find this place? Back at the compound, Dorothy had only managed to narrow the location of the burial site down to two possibilities: the enormous city of Damascus and the Orontes River, which stretched for over one hundred and fifty miles. Finding our exact location was nothing short of impossible. Yet somehow they had found me. With only two of them against an army of at least fifty Architects, they were outmatched and in serious trouble. Why hadn't they waited for a better opportunity to reveal themselves?

Baeloc seemed only puzzled for a moment, but it faded quickly, and his excitement grew for the chance to kill his enemies. Pointing a finger toward Dorothy and Abelish, he avidly issued a command.

"Run!" I shouted. Dorothy and Abelish either didn't hear me or didn't care. The Architects pulled out their weapons and raced toward them. Then I realized why my friends looked so confident. Clutched in Abelish's hands was a familiar sight.

Adino's spear.

Abelish had reconnected the spearhead. Neither he

nor Dorothy had ever used the weapon before out of fear of what the spear could do. But if ever there were a time to test it, they had picked a good one. The Architects didn't understand the significance of the weapon and never faltered as they swarmed toward them. Dorothy dove away from Abelish and looked at me.

"Get on the ground now!" she ordered.

The instruction was meant for only my ears, and I didn't hesitate to dive face-first into the dirt and cover my head with my hands. Baeloc understood the order at the last minute and dove on the ground as well as Abelish thrust the spear toward the oncoming wave of Architects.

Everything fell silent for what felt like an eternity. No sounds. I couldn't even hear my own pulse or my rapid breathing. Too afraid to look directly at the weapon, I waited for the silence to end and prayed it hadn't backfired. Without warning, a white light shot out of the tip of the spear, and the Architects staggered to a stop. The spotlight burst, and the glass in the church windows and in the remaining SUVs showered onto the ground. A tremendous sound shook my body, rocking it back and forth as the light surged, growing to a blinding brightness. For the second time in less than a few hours, I blacked out completely.

25

"What the heck happened here?" Trendon's voice brought me back from unconsciousness. With surprising care, he pulled me up into a sitting position and patted me on the back as I desperately tried to shake away the vertigo. "I seriously leave you for like fifteen minutes, and look at the mess you make."

My head throbbed. Unable to blink the white light from my eyes, I feared the flash from the spear had permanently damaged my retinas. "It wasn't me," I whimpered. "Adino." I couldn't seem to catch my breath but repeated the name. "Adino."

"Who?" Trendon asked.

"The spear." Slowly, I turned and saw the motionless body of Baeloc lying prostrated on the ground. "Is he . . . dead?" I asked.

"Don't know yet," Trendon said, continuing to steady me with his hand. "But we probably shouldn't wait around to find out."

I still felt too dizzy to stand up, but Trendon had

a point. If I had survived the blast, there was a good chance so had Baeloc. "Where are the others?"

"What others?"

"The Architects?" There had been over fifty of them charging toward Abelish, but only Baeloc remained.

Trendon glanced around the area and puffed out his cheeks. "You got me. There's still a whole bunch of them back at the mansion."

The events before I blacked out replayed in my mind. Abelish had used the spear against the Architects, and the result had been a mighty blast of energy. Now they were gone. I looked into Trendon's eyes, and his blurry image swirled in front of my face.

"Abelish used it. He used the . . . wait, are you wearing a headband?"

He had finally come into focus, and the unusual accessory of tattered fabric tied above his ears distracted my concentration.

Trendon blushed. "Oh, yeah, that. I just thought since it was like a war zone, I'd try it, but you don't like it?"

"No," I said flatly, shaking my head.

"Right." He quickly yanked the headband off. "It was crazy back there. The whole mansion has burned to the ground."

I looked south toward Baeloc's fortress. The sky glowed orange from the fire, and a billowing cloud of smoke rose above the tree line.

"Temel?" I asked.

Trendon nodded. "Did you really have to guess?"

I knew the explosion had been Temel's handiwork. No one else had the ability to make a Fourth of July fireworks show look more like a bunch of sparklers. In the distance, I could faintly hear the sound of machine guns firing.

"Who's still shooting?" I asked.

"Sherez and some of the other good guy Architects," Trendon said, making his fingers into quotations, "are fighting the other dudes. It was nuts!"

"How did you get here?"

He scratched the back of his neck and pointed to an idling van, where Cabarles sat behind the wheel, looking anxious. "Joseph showed up and untied us."

"Joseph?" The name took a moment to register. "He's here?"

Trendon nodded toward the church, and I saw Joseph trying to revive Dorothy. Seeing my teacher lying almost lifeless jolted me fully awake. I raced over to her and helped Joseph sit her up on the ground.

"Hey," Joseph said.

"Hey," I answered. At the moment, that would have to do for a greeting. Dorothy looked really battered. She had been standing the closest to Abelish when he had swung the spear. Her eyes were open, but they had a glazed look, and her breathing sounded slow and erratic.

"Don't try to move," I said, but if she understood me, she made no acknowledgment. A stream of saliva dangled from her mouth, and I wiped it with my sleeve. I had never seen her in such poor condition. It worried me that the blast had somehow left her catatonic. "Dorothy!"

I spoke loudly next to her ear and squeezed her shoulders. "Can you hear me?"

She mumbled something incoherent and then suddenly released a harsh fit of coughing. "Oh, my head!" she said as her eyes regained their focus and she covered her temples with her fingers.

"Can we move her?" I asked Joseph.

"She's in bad shape, but I guess we better," Joseph muttered. "She's not as bad as him though."

I followed Joseph's gaze and felt my spirits drop. Abelish lay next to the church in a crumpled heap. With Dorothy somewhat reviving, I ran to his aid.

"Abelish, are you . . . ?" The sight of the fallen warrior prevented me from finishing my sentence. His eyes were open, blinking slowly, but his vision seemed distant and focused elsewhere. At first he didn't appear to be breathing, but then I faintly heard the soft sound of air filling his lungs. The explosion had singed most of the robes on his upper body, exposing his chest and abdomen. I covered my mouth in shock, not because of the hundreds of leprous lesions dotting his skin, but due to the gruesome burns above his stomach and covering his palms. The painful marks had been burned in the shape of the spear.

Abelish finally noticed me, and his eyes widened. "The spear?" he asked in a hoarse whisper. "Where's the spear?"

With tears streaming from my eyes, I searched the ground for the weapon. Figuring Abelish may have dropped it after the explosion, I looked toward the church, but there was no sign of the spear anywhere.

"It's not here," I said, returning to his side. "Do you remember where you left it?"

His blackened hand closed around my wrist. "Then it is destroyed." He closed his eyes as his breathing steadied. "Good. That is good."

In the same mysterious manner the army of Architects had vanished, Adino's spear had done the same. One could only guess what had happened, but I imagined the massive amount of energy released from the untested weapon had caused them to disintegrate.

"Oh geez!" Trendon said, kneeling down next to me. "What happened to him?"

"He swung Adino's spear and destroyed the Architects," I answered.

Trendon didn't seem to understand for a moment, but then gaped at Abelish in disbelief. "He used it? The one from Dorothy's compound? With the spearhead? Did you see it?" Abelish startled and glared up at Trendon disapprovingly. "Probably not the best time to ask that, huh?" Trendon asked. "Hey, we need to get out of here."

I looked over my shoulder and saw Joseph supporting Dorothy as she limped toward the van. Cabarles stood by the back door, urging them forward.

"Can we move you?" Trendon asked Abelish.

Abelish licked his lips but then shook his head. "The artifact did what we thought it would do. The power in that weapon filled me with such brilliant force. I knew nothing could harm me if I swung it, and I had been right. But now I am broken on the inside." He sputtered a cough and sighed. "I don't wish to move. Go help Dorothy and leave me be."

"We're not leaving you," I said. "That's out of the question."

"I will not blame you. I want to rest. Let me be at peace."

"Let's go, guys!" Joseph yelled from the back of the vehicle.

I stood with Trendon, and the two of us stared down at the battered warrior. He had to know more about his condition than any of us. Judging by the nasty mark across his midsection, the spear may have caused internal damage, and I couldn't begin to imagine the pain he felt. Regardless of his wishes, I knew I couldn't leave him just lying there out in the open. That was the sort of cruel behavior reserved for the Architects, not for us.

"I'm sorry, Abelish, but we're not listening to you. Trendon, can you help me lift him up? But be careful of his burns."

Trendon didn't object, and despite knowing of Abelish's disease, he slid his hands under the warrior's back and helped me hoist him to his feet. Abelish groaned in pain, and his chest heaved as we started walking to the van.

Cabarles helped carry Abelish into the middle of the vehicle and then hopped back into the driver's seat. Even though most of the people seated in the eight-passenger van were incapacitated, I still felt safe being surrounded once again by my friends. I seriously thought I would never see any of them again.

"Wait!" Trendon stopped me from climbing in the back. "What about the artifact?"

Elijah's Fire.

Baeloc still had it in his possession, and we would have to retrieve it from him. We turned to look for Baeloc, but he no longer lay in a heap on the ground. Instead, the Architect shakily stood on his feet, holding the artifact above his head. I could see his lips moving, but I couldn't hear any sounds. The air had become saturated with a pungent smell like burned plastic, filling my nostrils. That was when I noticed the ax's blade had changed colors. The once burned metal now glowed bright orange. Thunder clapped as the sky transformed into a black mixture of activity, churning mysteriously in the heavens. It was unexplainable. It looked as though some mammoth giant, hiding in the sky directly above the burial site, had begun to blend together the clouds with an enormous spoon. A strong wind picked up, hurling dirt, leaves, and twigs against the windshield.

"Get out of the car!" Dorothy shouted.

Joseph and Cabarles dove from the front seats, and Dorothy staggered out the opposite side. Trendon yanked my arm back through the door, and the two of us barely had enough time to pull Abelish from the middle seats when the unthinkable happened. As if the awesome display of brewing clouds wasn't enough to leave us speechless, a cylindrical bolt of lightning formed suddenly and began twirling and spiraling serpent-like within the cloud formation.

Though his voice was drowned out by the tumultuous wind, Baeloc's mouth continued to move as he spoke his commands. Then the lightning bolt released and came screaming down toward the van. The pillar of fire struck the roof, exploding with a firework of bright light, and within seconds completely engulfed the vehicle. The fire scorched everything—glass, metal, upholstery—and the tires all turned into smoldering ash.

Holding up my hands, I tried to shield my face as my eyes stung and my hair seemed as though it too would catch fire and burn me into oblivion. Standing that close to the blaze should've killed everyone, but the unnatural fire seemed to only destroy whatever it touched. Just like in the Bible when Elijah called down the fire to consume the priests of Baal, he had survived. If we could somehow avoid the flames, we could survive, but with Baeloc controlling the artifact, no place would be safe.

Suddenly, Trendon was behind me, dragging me away from the blaze. Dorothy and the others gathered around me as Joseph dropped an object in my hands. Though wrapped in fabric, I recognized its shape and its familiar weight. Somehow, he had stolen back the Tebah Stick from the mansion. Bewildered, I stared at him, trying to figure out how he could've found it.

"No time!" he shouted, shaking his head.

Cabarles pulled me in close and spoke next to my ear. "Don't let them control you!" I could barely hear him say as the gale-like winds increased in volume. "You are their master! Not the other way around!"

There was no time to discuss it further. Baeloc still stood in the road, extending the ax as another bolt of lightning formed in the clouds.

Slipping my hands under the fabric, I grabbed hold of the Tebah Stick, and the disharmony in my mind instantly became clear. A humming sensation generating from the artifact tickled my fingertips and then worked its way through the rest of my body.

The Shomehr were closer than I had initially believed. Glancing around the burial site, I saw them standing close to the church as though they had simply appeared. The fog still lingered, obscuring their faces from view, but by the way their bodies stood hunched, I knew they were ready to pounce.

Release us. They spoke in my mind. *We shall punish him for you.*

I felt so much power. Absolute control. If I wanted it, the Shomehr would do whatever I asked of them. They were six powerful creatures at my command. With the Tebah Stick in my possession, I would never have to fear anything in the world. The creatures could provide me total protection, but that wasn't all. They could be summoned to carry out any task, no matter how great or bizarre. Wealth. Security. Maybe even immortality. I could rule the world with them as my servants, and no one would ever oppose me.

All of these ideas manifested in my mind, and I knew the Tebah Stick would deliver the same power and control to me whenever I held it.

He is nothing compared to our strength. We shall rip him limb from limb. Their voices linked together into one, but as I listened to them speak, I realized it was my voice I heard in my head, not some echoing monsters! Hearing the familiar tone scared me more than facing Baeloc. The ideas of power had come from them, planted in my mind to convince me to use them in whatever way I saw fit. But that would be wrong. No one deserved such power. The Shomehr were trying to take control of me, and Cabarles had warned me they would. I had to prove I was their master.

"Don't kill him!" I ordered.

Let us kill him! They demanded. *Let us kill!*

"No!" I shouted. I faced the creatures and willed myself to show no signs of fear. "Do as I say!"

In doing this, Baeloc saw the creatures too. Abandoning his attention on my friends, the Architect directed the next bolt of fire toward the Shomehr. The air around the burial site crackled and fizzed with electricity as the night once more glowed with blinding light. The creatures had barely enough time to dive out of the way as the fire hit the ground where they had been standing and lit the side of the church ablaze.

"Amber! Be careful!" I didn't know who the voice belonged to, but they needed to not distract me.

"Be quiet!" I hissed and then focused my thoughts on the creatures. "Take the ax from him and then bring him to me."

The Shomehr made no verbal response, but I knew they understood. My mind couldn't process the sheer speed of the creatures as they charged on all fours toward their target. The triumphant look in Baeloc's eyes turned to one of panic as he scrambled backward, still clinging to the artifact and rambling off his commands. Another bolt of fire formed rapidly and struck the ground in front of him. All of the Shomehr separated from the group, but one of them lost its balance. Violently the creature clawed the ground, but its momentum had reached too great a speed, and it tumbled into the fire.

The remaining five Shomehr watched as the flames dispersed, leaving behind a small pile of ash where their brother had once stood. All at once they joined together, and their voices, like the haunting cries of a mourning woman, filled the air. The sound of it froze me on the inside as I recalled the chilling howls I had heard from Mt. Arayat. At the time I didn't know why they made such awful sounds, but being in control of the Tebah Stick, I could understand their pain, their sadness, and their anger.

Once more they homed in on Baeloc, only now they seemed wary of his ability. I remembered how in the cave, Trendon had kept the Shomehr away momentarily with a road flare and rubbing alcohol. The blaze from the road flare had been insignificant, especially when compared to what Elijah's Fire could produce, yet it had held the creatures at bay long enough to give us time to find the Tebah Stick. Perhaps the Shomehr didn't understand fire, having been imprisoned in the mountain for thousands of years without any means of light or warmth. I also knew the fear would not keep them from carrying out my command. Like a hunting pack of wolves, they surrounded Baeloc. Above the Architect, another massive pillar of fire had formed in the clouds, one easily dwarfing the other bolts in size. When the creatures saw the overwhelming display, they cowered away from Baeloc, no longer wanting anything to do with his power.

"Stop!" I demanded. "Stop him!"

The faintest hint of a smile formed on Baeloc's lips. His eyes looked at mine and then fell upon the Tebah Stick as his smile widened. Speaking in his incoherent language, his voice rose until he practically snarled his instructions. I knew what was about to happen, but I was powerless against it. As my eyes drifted upward, the massive bolt of fire released from the clouds and fell toward me.

From my peripheral, I could see several of the creatures racing toward me. But the fire, now lighting up the heavens with beautiful orange and crimson light was falling at too great a speed. One of the Shomehr reached me first and propelled my body backward, knocking the wind from my lungs with its force. The others arrived a tad too late. With my mind still whirling after the hit from the creature, I managed to look as the fire consumed three of the Shomehr. Like their brother before, only ash remained.

Muscular hands stood me to my feet, and I could feel the presence of the creature standing behind me. It made no attempt to charge at Baeloc, and I assumed seeing the others devoured by the flames had quenched all of its desires to attack. But the Architect still controlled Elijah's Fire. Baeloc looked furious as he kept his eyes trained on the creature at my back, daring it to move. His lips once again formed the words necessary for commanding the fire, but then he stopped suddenly and swallowed.

The sixth monster stood directly behind him. It had waited for the fire to strike and had crept up to Baeloc without him knowing. Before the Architect could react, the creature struck, slicing its claws through Baeloc's wrist. Baeloc howled in pain and collapsed, dropping the artifact to the ground. The creature wasn't finished. Releasing a deafening moan, it fell upon Baeloc and pulled its claw back behind its head.

"Please," I whispered, squeezing the Tebah Stick tightly in my hands. "Don't kill him."

For a moment it resisted and brought its hand back farther as it prepared to deliver a fatal strike. Baeloc's death would be justified. He intended to destroy the world as payback and had no reservations about killing every human being. For that reason alone, he should be killed, and I was in a position to end it. I truly believed it would be a necessary killing, but I also replayed the conversation with Cabarles over and over in my mind. A fifteen-year-old girl had no business delivering that sort of judgment.

"Do as I say," I said. "Bring me the artifact, but don't let him escape."

Surrendering, the Shomehr lowered its hand and closed its fingers around Baeloc's throat. While it kept the Architect pinned against the ground, the other Shomehr retrieved the ax from where it had fallen and delivered it into my hands.

The fight was over.

26

The stone box still lay overturned where Baeloc had stood. Pieces of ash-covered glass littered the ground and crunched beneath my feet as I picked up the box and carefully placed the ax inside. Cabarles proved to be the only one brave enough to move close to the Shomehr. The creature watched him apprehensively as he knelt beside Baeloc and pressed the tip of Dorothy's gun into the Architect's chest.

"I believe I can handle it from here," he whispered, nodding at me. I nodded back and, closing my eyes, released the Shomehr from their command. The one that had brought me the ax turned and fled into the forest behind the church. But the one holding Baeloc's throat lingered for a moment and lowered its head until its fog-covered face hovered only inches away from the Architect's. Baeloc's jaw clinched tight as he stared defiantly up at the creature. But then he suddenly released a terrified scream. Even I, with my connection to the Shomehr's thoughts, had no idea where the scream came from. His screaming continued for several moments until finally the creature released his grip and climbed off of him. Baeloc's whole body trembled, and his fingers clutched at his throat.

When the last Shomehr disappeared behind the church, I knew they were gone, but not completely. While I still held the Tebah Stick, they could easily be summoned to return.

"What was that all about?" Trendon asked me. "Why did he scream like that?"

"I don't know," I said, too exhausted to discuss it further.

Dorothy had helped Abelish lie on the ground, and like the Architect, he too trembled, but not from fear. The crushing pain inside of Abelish had reached an excruciating level.

"How is he?" I handed Dorothy the stone box. She took it in her hands but didn't reach for the Tebah Stick. It made no difference. There was no way I would let anyone else take hold of it until we were far away from the mansion.

"He's not going to make it. His injuries are too deep." She was crying, but there was also a look of understanding in her eyes. I cried as well as I realized Abelish had finally fulfilled his destiny.

"Amber," Abelish whispered. "You are a brave warrior."

Did having the misfortune of being the only one in the world capable of controlling the Tebah Stick make me a warrior? I didn't think so, but I didn't have the heart to say so to Abelish.

"Don't let him take . . ." Abelish tried to bring his hand up to muffle a cough, but the pain overtook him and tears fell from his eyes.

"Don't speak, Abelish." Dorothy leaned over and kissed him on his cheek. "We understand."

Watching the man writhe in pain and knowing his life lingered only inches away from death was almost unbearable. I glanced over my shoulder to where Cabarles still held Baeloc at gunpoint and realized an eerie similarity between the Architect and Abelish. Both men had lived their whole lives in misery. Their conditions had brought them years of embarrassment and pain, and they both had to live hiding from the outside world. Yet a mighty difference separated the two. Abelish fought for good while Baeloc chose evil. I wasn't sure what would happen to Baeloc in the end. Yes, he would be punished, but in what way? Imprisonment? He would live on, but Abelish would die. It didn't seem fair.

Once again it thundered above, but unlike the thunder that came from the artifact, this time rain fell upon our heads. At first it peppered the ground lightly but then turned into a torrential downpour. The fire still burning the northern wall of the church extinguished and released a satisfying hiss. I didn't mind the rain, and I looked at Trendon and Joseph standing next to each other, watching me in silence as I held Abelish's hand. The sound of whirling helicopter blades joined the thunder.

"Is that Temel?" I asked, pointing to the chopper in the distance.

"Let's hope so," Trendon said. "He's got Lisa with him."

"Lisa's here too?"

"She refused to stay behind," Dorothy said. "She was the one who figured out the location of the grave."

I hadn't given much thought to the strange appearance of Dorothy, Abelish, and Temel, when literally thousands of possibilities existed, but now I desperately needed to know. How did Lisa figure it out? That question would have to wait to be answered as Abelish's breathing began to slow.

"That's going to fill up fast," Trendon muttered, nodding at the burial site, where the rain poured into the hole. "Is there a way to cover the tomb? It seems kinda disrespectful not to. I wouldn't want Elisha to come haunt me for not keeping him dry."

Letting go of Abelish's hand, I stood quickly. Elisha's grave. I suddenly remembered something important about it. Normally the idea would've been too unbelievable to try, but my grasp on reality had weakened as of late. I had just seen fire falling from heaven and had used a scepter to control mysterious creatures. Cabarles had told me whenever I felt evil had completely surrounded me I just needed to believe. Well, maybe, just maybe, it could work.

"Quick! Everyone help me!" I shouted.

"What do you want us to do?" Joseph looked at Trendon, who merely shrugged his shoulders.

"Help me carry him to the grave!"

"Amber, he's too weak," Dorothy reasoned. "Why do you want us . . ."

"Don't argue with me. Just do it!" I snapped. We needed to move fast.

Abelish coughed and groaned in protest as the four of us hefted his weight and hurried over to the scaffolding. Cabarles kept his concentration on Baeloc but watched us with a curious expression on his face.

With Trendon on one side of the ladder and myself on the other, we held Abelish's feet as Joseph and Dorothy slowly lowered him from above. The ladder rungs felt slick and dangerous, but we descended, feeling the weight of Abelish's body in our arms.

"What are we doing?" Trendon asked. "Are you all right?"

"Shhh! Don't ask me just yet."

"But, Amber . . ."

"Please!" I didn't want to jinx the moment.

When we arrived almost to the bottom, my feet sank into the mud. Bracing my back against the ladder, I steadied my body and held on. We were almost there when I heard Dorothy start to sob.

"Oh, Abelish." The warrior's chest no longer moved, and I felt his legs go limp.

"No! We need more time!" I screamed. "Don't stop!" I could tell my friends thought I'd lost it, but I didn't care. We had to try. "Help me lower him into the grave!"

Though their faces revealed their skepticism, they did as I told them.

"Why are we doing this?" Joseph asked as he brushed some of my wet hair out of my eyes and placed his hands on my shoulders. "We can't help him now. Abelish is dead."

"I know," I answered. "I know. But we just . . . I just need to see something!"

"What do you need to see?"

"Remember the story of the Israelites?" I asked. Joseph shook his head in confusion. "It was in the books you sent me."

"Books?" He licked his lips. "I don't know what you're talking about."

"I know it was you, Joseph. The first and second books of Kings. The two leather-bound books you stuck in my mailbox at school. You can tell me the truth!" But Joseph's eyes told the real story. He hadn't sent me the books either. I had made the mistake about Dorothy and now him.

"Well, if *you* didn't send them . . ." I felt utterly confused.

"Never mind who sent the books!" Trendon shouted. "What happened to the Israelites?"

I wiped the water from my face and stared at Trendon. "Don't you remember? We both read about it. After Elisha had been dead for over a year, some Israelites brought another dead man to the grave. When they lowered his body onto Elisha's bones . . ."

Trendon's eyes widened, and everyone stared at the grave as Abelish sat up.

Dorothy gasped and pressed her hand against her chest. "Abelish?"

Abelish blinked and looked skyward, his nostrils flaring with every breath he took. It was at that moment I realized something miraculously different about him.

Yes, he had revived and had adequate strength to move and breathe, but I also noticed his skin had healed. All of the lesions and the marks of his leprosy had vanished. Even in the near complete darkness of the grave, I could see the healthy color in his face and arms.

"My goodness!" Abelish said, looking down at his hands and flexing his fingers. "I feel really, really good."

Trendon wrapped his arms around me and squeezed me in a massive bear hug.

27

The Orontes River looked like a glowing silver worm stretching for miles beneath the helicopter. Temel sat at the controls wearing a thick, padded headset through which he conversed with Dorothy seated next to him. He also wore his trademark sunglasses despite flying under a dark horizon and chewed gleefully on a toothpick. From time to time, he would glance back, smile, and shake his head in disbelief, no doubt trying to understand how a couple of kids had managed to save the world . . . again.

I sat between Lisa and Trendon with my head resting on Trendon's shoulder while Joseph sat across from us, staring down at the river and hardly speaking. Abelish, Cabarles, and the rest of Dorothy's men had stayed behind to clean up the mess and ensure Baeloc had plenty of security. Sherez and the other rebellious Architects promised to help, but Dorothy had given Abelish the charge to avoid using their services at all costs. She didn't trust any of them, and I didn't blame her. Many of the

Architects still loyal to Baeloc had escaped, and I knew we hadn't seen the last of them, but for the moment, we were safe.

Abelish had looked amazing and even unwrapped his turban to show off his handsome salt and pepper gray hair before we embarked on our helicopter ride back to Dorothy's compound. Elisha's grave had breathed into him a new sense of purpose and a new chance in life. What he would do with it was still a mystery, but he promised to make sure all was well before he left. I couldn't have been happier for him.

At first I worried about Baeloc. There had been too many mistakes made with him and the artifacts, but I felt differently now knowing Cabarles and Abelish were personally taking charge. I trusted those men with my life and knew they had everything under control. As for the artifacts, they rested in a locked, steel case at Dorothy's feet. They needed to be analyzed, and after the incident with Adino's spear, Dorothy wanted to take extra precaution when it finally came to destroy them. I stared at the case often and wondered about the Shomehr. Were they somewhere down below, racing along the river and trying to keep up with the helicopter? Would they still haunt my dreams even though I had released them?

Though difficult to hear because of the roaring blades of the helicopter, I leaned in close to Lisa and spoke into her ear.

"How did you do it?" I asked. "How did you find us? I didn't think I'd ever see any of you again." The arrival of my friends to Baeloc's mansion was one of the most miraculous events of all. There had been no way to find us, yet Lisa figured it out on her own. Not that she wasn't capable of brilliant things. I just had to know.

"The numbers," Lisa shouted back. The Orontes River vanished beneath us as the helicopter continued south. Flat desert with the occasional cluster of lights from small cities made up the scenery. "The ones you wrote down back at the compound."

"What numbers?" I asked, flinching with confusion. I couldn't remember writing any numbers down.

"The next morning, after you and Trendon were kidnapped, everyone was in a state of panic. I had never seen Dorothy so angry. She kept yelling at everyone and crying. We all tried to help, but no one had any idea where to begin to look for you. So I went through your things back in your bedroom, and the numbers kind of stood out to me. You left them with your books by your backpack."

"I still don't know what you're talking about. I didn't write any numbers down." Lisa had to have made a bizarre mistake. Someone else must have written the numbers because I felt positive it wasn't me.

"Yes you did. Don't you remember? When the three of us were researching in the conference room, you wrote down the numbers of the verses in those leather-bound books of yours."

My eyes widened as I finally remembered. "Oh yeah, I remember, but those were just my notes. I didn't mean to write those down, and I certainly didn't think they would help anyone."

"My dad's a pilot," Lisa continued. "He's shown me from time to time how to plot travel plans for his jet using latitude and longitude. You wrote 3:5, 8, 3:6, and 4:5. When I saw them written on the paper, I realized they looked just like mapping coordinates. I found a travel website on Dorothy's computer, plugged in the numbers, and bingo. *35 degrees, 8 north, 36 degrees, 45 east.* Those happen to be the exact coordinates of Hama City, Syria. Dorothy knew I was right as soon as I told her, and we found you guys, probably just in time."

I sat, staring dumbfounded at Lisa. Mapping coordinates. The numbers were linked to latitude and longitude. Not in a million years would I have ever made the connection. Lisa's brilliance had saved our lives. Sitting back in my seat, I ran my hands through my hair, still blown away by how she had figured it out. If Lisa hadn't flown with us to Jordan, Trendon, Cabarles, and I would probably be dead by now.

One thing was for certain: the circled verses in those books linking to the precise location of Hama City, Syria, had been no coincidence. Someone had tried to send me a message. But who? My two guesses of Dorothy and Joseph had been wrong. It made sense though, since neither one of them had ever seen Baeloc's mansion and they couldn't have known the coordinates. It had to be someone close to Baeloc. Someone on the inside. A spy, maybe, or one of the rebellious Architects. But Sherez didn't know, and his followers only showed up to help when Dorothy and Abelish arrived. It couldn't have been them either. Whoever it was, they had been to Roland

and Tesh and had dropped the leather books into my mailbox. I swallowed as I finally came to a realization and remembered some of the last words Kendell Jasher had said to me back at Papa B's restaurant.

I know things Dorothy doesn't. Codes, numbers, coordinates . . .

At the time, those words had confused me, but now I understood. Jasher had been the one, and he had even dropped a hint to me. It had been one of his final acts before Baeloc killed him. He had to have known his life was in danger and felt he needed to send word to someone. But why not Dorothy or even his own flesh and blood? I looked at Joseph, but he didn't notice me staring at him as he watched the ground passing beneath the helicopter. Of all the people he could've warned, Jasher chose me. It was as though the pieces of a difficult puzzle had finally fit together. I couldn't even begin to wrap my brain around it, but then the words of encouragement Cabarles had spoken to me back at Baeloc's mansion returned to my memory.

Fear not. For they that be with us are more than they that be with them.

He had been right all along, and I would be foolish to think everything had happened by only luck.

Temel landed the helicopter just west of Amman, and by the time we arrived at Dorothy's compound, the sun had risen for the morning. We each showered, changed into clean clothes, and met together in one of the conference rooms for breakfast.

"I know this may come as a shocker to everyone, but I'm starving!" Trendon said, plopping down in a chair and snatching a fork in his hand.

"Me too," I agreed. "I wonder what we're having."

"Breakfast burritos," Temel answered, entering through the door. He dropped a large paper sack on the table, and we all leaned close to breathe in the delicious aroma.

"Breakfast burritos for real? You can get that sort of stuff here in Amman?" Trendon asked.

Temel shrugged as we each snagged an aluminum-foil-wrapped burrito. Eggs, cheese, bacon, and sausage all encased in a piping hot tortilla were the perfect combination for breakfast, and I ate almost half of mine with two mammoth bites. Temel didn't seem too excited about the meal and instead squirted a tiny packet of hot sauce into his mouth.

"You're not eating?" Lisa asked.

"Nah, I don't like burritos."

"But I thought you were from Mexico," Trendon said through a mouthful of food.

"Psh! I'm not from Mexico." Temel shook his head and stepped back out of the room.

"What?" Trendon asked when Lisa and I glared at him. "Do you know where he's from?"

I looked at Lisa as we both chewed and realized we had no idea where the mysterious Temel called home.

Dorothy pushed open the door, and Joseph followed her into the room. His backpack rested on his shoulders, and he looked as though he were ready to leave for a long trip.

"You're leaving?" I stood from my seat.

"Yep," Joseph said as he unwrapped the foil from one of the remaining burritos and took a bite.

"Why would you leave? Where will you go?" I looked at Lisa, who shared my confused expression. Trendon glanced at Joseph but didn't say anything in response. Joseph was just a fifteen-year-old kid like us. There were limitations of what we could and couldn't do. He couldn't just go backpacking across a foreign country.

"I've got plenty of places to go," Joseph answered with a shrug. "My uncle has property all over the world, and he's left me a ton of money. I'll be fine."

"Joseph, you should stay for a while. Just until things clear," Dorothy said, sitting in one of the empty spaces at the table.

He considered her suggestion as he chewed but then shook his head. "No, I don't think that's a good idea."

"You could come back to school with us," Lisa suggested.

Trendon muffled a laugh and smiled at Joseph apologetically. The gesture didn't appear to offend Joseph, since he chuckled lightly as well.

"School? I don't think so."

"But you can't just skip school forever. You're not even old enough to drop out!" I said. Joseph was acting irrationally.

"I'm just taking a break for a little while. I'll go back soon. Besides, I've been living with my uncle for almost a year now, and I haven't gone to school once. No one misses me. They don't even know I exist."

Scooting my seat back, I walked up to him and squeezed his arm. "That's not true, and you know it. We know you exist. You're one of us, and we want you to stay."

A pained look formed in Joseph's eyes as he stared into mine and then once more he looked at Trendon. I didn't understand what that look meant. Was he still hurting for the loss of his uncle, or did he feel he had done too much to us and could never be fully accepted as our friend?

"You know, Joseph, we're going to try to find the last Weapon of Might, and we could use your help," Dorothy said. "You've proven to be quite resourceful, and that could come in handy with our search."

He smiled but gave a firm pull on his backpack straps to finalize his decision. "I'll be around if you really need me," he whispered. He nodded at Trendon and turned to leave.

"Later, Joe," Trendon said as Joseph left the room.

I hesitated for a moment but couldn't keep myself from charging after him.

"Wait!" I said, catching up with him and pulling on his backpack. "Why are you doing this? You don't have to leave. We forgive you of everything, and I trust you now." Is that what he wanted to hear? Because I really did trust him. He had risked his life to help us.

"It's not that. I'm just confused right now, and I need some time to be alone. My uncle was the only family I had, and now he's gone too. I don't mind it though. It'll be fun figuring things out on my own. And don't worry,

I'm sure we'll see each other again, and if I find anything that can help with Dorothy's search on the final artifact, I'll call you. I think I can find your number."

"We need you here," I said, but I had already released my hold on him and had taken a step back toward the room. There seemed to be no convincing him otherwise.

"You don't need me, Amber. I think you're already in good hands."

Without even a handshake or a hug good-bye, Joseph left me standing alone in Dorothy's compound. Figuring his departure would devastate me, I felt surprised when I didn't cry. I knew I'd miss him, but I wasn't necessarily worried about him. He had proven to do things better on his own, but I needed my friends to survive. Returning to the room, Trendon and Lisa stood and surrounded me.

"Is he gone?" Trendon asked, glancing over my shoulder toward the door.

"Yeah, he's gone."

"Are you all right?" Lisa asked.

I smiled and pulled the two of them into my arms. "Yep, I'm fine."

And at that exact moment, I knew Joseph was right.

I was already in good hands.

Acknowledgments

The list grows with every book. I'm grateful for the supporting cast of my wife, Heidi, and my kids, Jackson, Gavin, and Camberlyn. I was lucky to have been raised in a close-knit family who shares my love of stories. My parents have endured my exaggerations over the years and encouraged me in my pursuit of this dream.

I want to thank those who helped with the creation of my upcoming projects: Jennifer Judd, Ethan Judd, Michael Cole, Tyler Whitesides, Jared Weight, Kevin Lemley, Jeff Miller, Taylor Fleming, B.K. Bostick, and Kevin Wille. I really appreciate your contributions. There are more out there, and I am truly grateful for all you do.

I love Cedar Fort! They've been so good to me and have surrounded my books with enthusiastic people. Thank you to Lyle, Jennifer, Heidi, Kelley, and Josh. My publishing experience with you has been a great blessing.

I want to acknowledge Mark McKenna, who created an awesome cover. You are amazing!

Last, and as always, I'd be nothing without my readers. Every email or letter I receive with questions or comments about my books boosts me to want to write more. I love your feedback, and I hope you'll continue to give my books a try. There will be many more, and I promise you I'll keep working to write them better and better.